The Night Out.

Chapter 1.

Jake gazed out of the window in the drab DWP office where he worked. Drizzle caused rivulets of water to snake their way down the pane. He concentrated hard on their journey to distract him from the ugly vision of Grimsby's dilapidated dockyards and the East Marsh district of the town. Had he gazed through the window opposite him, he would have seen a sunnier sky on the horizon, accentuating the greenery visible at a distance coming from the Bradley Woods area. But he didn't as this would have involved standing up and drawing attention to himself at a time when he seemed like he was at boiling point.

The office's colour scheme was multiple shades of beige. It was considered that grey appeared too dour, the DWP had opted for a colour scheme that appeared more 'homely' for their employees. Jake thought they missed the mark by a long shot. The sandy coloured desks framed by darker cork boards with identical sheets adorning each one. Any personalisation of work stations was prohibited in case people needed to 'hot desk', an unlikely scenario since the building had been haemorrhaging staff ever since the coalition government came into power. The walls lined with bottom-lighted framed pictures of what Jake was certain contained stock photos of 'business' people smiling.

Jake had been working at this DWP office for close to six years. He'd intended it on being a temporary situation, but with a global recession causing severe problems in the UK, jobs became scarce. Added to that fact, Grimsby was already a quagmire when it came to employment. He knew his options became narrower over time. He'd accepted the fact he would achieve nothing remotely resembling greatness and now wanted contentment. Sadly, contentment was nowhere to be found in this job, his own personal purgatory.

His job involved taking new claims to benefit, specifically ESA, the sickness benefit. Two years after starting the position, the government changed to a coalition between the Tories and the Liberals. Leaning politically to the left, Jake loathed the situation and with good reason. Changes began, demonising the ill and disabled in the country and he found his minor role in the DWP to be a cog in a machine leading the way to a new, media savvy, Nazi regime where the poor and needy were the targets. He hated himself for being part of this. He despised the fact he relied on the income and loathed the DWP as an institution. His sympathy for the circumstances that led people to his line was absolute, and it tore him up inside what hardships and pressures he had an awareness they faced.

Contrary to this, he despised talking to almost every person on the phone. He regarded most people he spoke to as idiots, having to endure spitefully racist diatribes such as, 'If I had a turban I'd get everything' on almost an hourly basis. His contempt for the wilful ignorance of some people seemingly knew no bounds, and he had not the patience nor the will to deal with it any longer. Most accents in the country had annoyed him as it was the most base and guttural drawls of these that he encountered. From the nasal 'errrhmmms' punctuating every sentence from the Scouse, to the sloppy 'oy' sounds that seemed to shape every word from the West Midlands denizens, his nerves constantly frayed, his day ranging from moods of great irritation to major rage. He told himself repeatedly that the 'customers' were people in need and that he was no better than any single one of them. The only time the callers seemed remotely decent often resulted in finding out they were terminally ill, which made Jake despair the notion that there was truly any cosmic justice. As he put it when ranting to friends, 'I spend most of my day dealing with cretins'.

This particular cretin he currently dealt with had now been on the phone for forty-five minutes to make a claim that usually took Jake twenty. The customer was afflicted by a spectacularly moronic sounding West Midlands accent. Jake had struggled to not hiss through clenched teeth the remarkably easy questions that caused this person so much difficulty. After the person had agreed to answer optional questions about his ethnic origin, Jake began his least favourite part of any call.

- Is your ethnic origin Asian, or Asian British. Black or Black British. Mixed ethnic group. Chinese or other ethnic group. White. Or prefer not to say?
- Oi'm jus' British mayte.
- No, that's not one of the options we can record. Imagine this is a claim form and we can just tick one of the boxes. Would you like me to repeat the options?
- Oi think thit moight be best mayte, yis.

Jake inwardly sighed and repeated the question. Only white people ever seemed to struggle with this one. He stated each option at a much slower pace.

- Yeah, Oi'm jus' British mayte.
- That's the answer you gave before. And I have already pointed out that isn't one of the options available. British is a nationality. Your ethnic origin is to do with which of those groups you identify with being. I'll go through each option with you one by one and you answer yes or no to each one and then we can move on OK?
- Roight you are my mayte.
- Ok so are you Asian, or Asian British?
- No.
- Are you Black, or Black British?
- Nyo.

'His accent is getting fucking worse' thought Jake bitterly.

- Are you of a mixed ethnic group?
- Nyow.
- Was that a no?

Sarcasm took hold of Jake's speech.

- Yis.
- Are you Chinese or 'other' ethnic group?
- No.
- Are you White?

Jake heavily emphasised the word white. 'I'll give the poor bastard a hint at least'

- No.

Jake was incredulous. He paused shaking his head and had the urge to sob. He couldn't see the person, but was 99% sure they were white as a lot of the 'nationalistic fucks' (as he frequently called them) in the country saw no difference between the word 'British' and 'White'

- Do you prefer not to say?
- No.
- That was all the options. Are you saying you don't fit into any of those categories?
- Oi down't rilly understand mayte.

Jake snapped back in a manner he would later describe as 'Basil Fawlty-esque'.

- OK. Right! So what we will do is put prefer not to say then shall we?

He gave no pause for the Black Country dweller to respond

- I mean, you don't have to answer them anyway and they mean absolutely zero, it's just here to waste everyone's time, anyway.

Despite his anger at the man's ignorance, Jake believed this to be true. He constantly questioned his managers why they had to ask about ethnic origin since all claims got dealt with over the phone so people were treated the same way. Not once in five years did they provide him with an answer and he genuinely did not know what caused his outrage more. He continued rapidly.

- There's another optional question here about disability. Let's skip that one as well shall we? Since you confused nationality with ethnicity, it's a safe bet that the notion of 'illness' and 'disability' are going to trip you up as well. That's it all done now. An hour well spent I'm sure you will agree. Have a nice day!
- Hauld on mayte, Oi jus' got won queshun.
- Yes. What is it?
- Whin do Oi get moi munnay?

Jake muted his phone and slammed his mouse controller down on the desk hard repeatedly in frustration. This caused many turned heads in the office and a wide smirk from his friend, Jim, sat opposite. He flicked the phone back on

- We have just. This second. Finished your claim form. I don't decide on whether you get benefits or not, as I mentioned earlier, you have to send a sick note in for your broken arm first as evidence.

The rest of the conversation was a fuzz in Jake's mind. The red mist had descended and his entire body was cramping through how aggravated he had become. As soon as the person ended the call, he threw his headset at the backboard of his station and stormed out of the room. His muscles were so tense that the act of opening the door resulted in a large slam into the wall, causing the door handle to make an indent in the plastering and crumbling plaster and brick dust to litter the floor. The stock photo shook and Jake swore that the fake smile wavered a little. Now everyone looked at him as he glanced back, slightly worried about the consequences of his temper.

- Door's fucked!

He weakly offered the first explanation his frazzled mind could think of. His line manager glowered at him across his desk. 'Cunt' thought Jake childishly as he bounded into the disabled toilets and tugged on his e-cigarette frantically. The act of vaping in a toilet not designated for him gave Jake a small amount of satisfaction at his puerile rebellion. With three hours to go, he contemplated saying he felt ill to leave although his absences were near enough at the limit before a warning gets issued. His annual leave ran out weeks ago and the only way he could get time off over the next eight months was to build up flexi-time by working extra.

After fifteen minutes of vaping, sat on the toilet with his pants round his ankles despite not using the toilet, he would try to brave it out. So paranoid was he about the DWP as an organisation, he always removed his trousers for these unauthorised breaks in case someone would burst in to catch him slacking off. This way, he could have plausible deniability. The rational side of him knew this would not happen as it grossly violates anyone's human rights. But he also knew managers here often exceeded their bounds under the guise of fake concern. Reluctantly, he pulled up his pants and flushed the empty toilet and trudged back to his desk. It was Friday, and he had now resolved to go out and get arseholed with Sarah from floor 3. She asked him earlier in the week and he was unsure, but now he was certain. He wanted to be awesome again in the way that only binge drinking could allow. Maybe with a side order of Charlie in case he got maudlin.

As he approached the desk he saw the now familiar brown envelope. A disciplinary letter. 'Christ, these fuckers were quick off the mark this time'. He weighed up his options. He was on a final written warning for various bullshit offences he never argued despite being farcical. This time, he couldn't deny he had a temper tantrum and had clearly done something wrong. No way out. 'Doctor's Monday', he planned, 'sick note, dismissal through illness with a pay-out is better than a sacking'.

Strangely, with the prospect of losing his job and the financial burden it carried, Jake felt better than he had done in years.

Chapter 2.

Pete parked his car on the pedestrian area outside the Barge Inn. He'd been coming here in his spare time for the best part of eight months ever since his brother, Jake went missing. His reasoning was that if Jake somehow turned up, then the Barge would likely to be somewhere he would show, being one of his favourite pubs for most of his life.

The string of bulbs on the outside the floating pub made it look festive. A lack of street lighting in this particular area of central Grimsby stressed the soft glow coming from outside the vessel, making it seem inviting; a beacon for the unrefreshed. Fond memories flooded through Pete's mind which he tried to suppress for fear of an emotional outburst that no-one would notice. He needed to remain strong.

Pete was almost physically the opposite from Jake. Whilst both men grew their hair long since an early age, a look attributed to the 80s metal scene that Jake loved, Pete stood over six foot and slender as opposed to the squat proportions of Jake who frequently skated the line between overweight and obese. Although bizarrely, they often got confused for one another by acquaintances, but never friends.

Friends and family told Pete that his constant searching was pointless and he should accept the fact that Jake would never come back. After reporting him as a missing person, less than a month later his mother stated she 'knew' he'd taken his own life and started to hysterically blame herself. His father quickly followed suit as all noticed a severe change in him over the past ten years. Jake was, at one point, an outgoing and gregarious individual. He used to attract new friends like flies and was what most would refer to as 'the life of the party'. This changed after his last relationship and his job at the DWP. He became withdrawn, spent most of his time indoors and would bitterly criticise almost everything. His previous boundless optimism replaced by a sneering cynicism that often threatened to infect everyone around him.

There'd been no funeral, as Jake could not be declared legally dead until seven years passed. Besides, there remained nothing to burn or bury, anyway. It had been suggested by various counsellors they hold a service to give everyone 'closure', but Pete resisted with uncharacteristic aplomb. There was a part of him that KNEW his brother to still be alive somewhere and his mood often changed regarding this notion from panic to fear and to anger, as if selfishly, Jake just hid himself away with no regards for anyone that cared for him.

Two months after Jake's disappearance, Pete battled a lettings agency for Jake's possessions. They had unsympathetically stated their plans to auction them off to cover loss of rent for the vacated flat and Pete stormed into the letting agency and taken the keys-almost by force-from an employee there with threats of violence never before used in his twenty-eight years. Pete moved all of Jake's belongings into a spare room in his recently-purchased house and spent hours meticulously combing them for some kind of clue to where his brother may be.

Frustratingly to Pete, he found himself unable to put into words why he so strongly felt his brother was still alive. His girlfriend, whilst sympathetic, had been vocal about how he needed to 'move on' and accept what everyone else did. The person who always used to help him find the words to explain himself was Jake. And he wasn't around to help.

Pete gazed at the Autumnal shedding of the leaves from the trees along the riverhead area of Grimsby. A seemingly endless supply always fell for around a month in September, making the entire area treacherous to walk on when it rained. He remembered the day when Jake took a piss in the river on a night out and slid down the embankment into the Freshney because of those 'bastard' leaves. Jake then deliberately pissed himself as he claimed 'Fuck it, I'm wet already'. Jake walked home as he lived only a few minutes away. He then showered, changed and returned to drinking again in less than forty-five minutes. He smiled at the memory, the 'old' Jake always seemed to come out when drunk or high.

Every memory he had of his brother was clear as if it happened yesterday, apart from one. The last time they ever spoke. Jake called him on the night he'd gone missing and the conversation seemed fuzzy. He knew the context of their words was Jake trying to get Pete to come out, but the actual content of what he said eluded him. Sometimes, Pete thought he was being belligerently badgered, other times, begged, and worst of all to him, that his sibling sounded sad, resigned and hurt that he wouldn't come. The grief counsellor stated that this was his mind playing tricks on him out of guilt, but that didn't sit right with Pete. Guilt wasn't the issue, just something was... wrong.

He started his car and left for home. Pete still needed to go to work in the morning and his employer showed no empathy in regard to his situation at all. He'd used all of his leave when the initial search began and now burnt-out took over as he'd worked seven months solid without a break and none in sight until his 'leave year' started again in two months. Taking time off sick was out of the question as paying bills and mortgage proved impossible on Statutory Sick Pay of eighty-two pounds per week. He resolved to drive a couple of laps around the town centre, now his ritual on these evening searches. As he reversed out of position, he spotted Jim, a mutual friend of him and his brother in the rear view mirror. They hadn't spoken to each other in over six months now. He couldn't put his finger on as to why. But now wasn't the time to change that.

Chapter 3.

- Where to mate?

Jake admired the interior of the taxi. The fresh leather and plastic scent referred to as 'new car smell' hit him first, but the immaculate and bright interior, no doubt valeted to perfection, came as a shock to him. Many taxis in this area stank of stale tobacco or beaten up old family cars used now to ferry lazy people and drunkards for extra income.

- Matrix club in town, please.

Jake had opted to sit in the back of the cab. He hated doing this as it reeked of a 'master and slave' dichotomy he despised. Although he felt that on this occasion, it seemed more out of respect for the plush interior, that if he sat in the front, he would somehow pollute the obvious pride and joy of this taxi driver.

On the in-car CD player, the familiar riff of Skid Row's 'Slave to The Grind' began. Jake's spirits lifted. A firm favourite of his from the age of fifteen, he had many fond memories of his first forays into Grimsby's nightlife, repeatedly putting this and several other tracks on the Jukebox in both the Barge and Lloyds Arms (now referred to as Old Lloyds) every single time he drank in those pubs.

-Tune! This is rare! Last sort of thing I'd expect to hear in a taxi!

Jake enthused to the taxi driver. The driver grinned in appreciation and allowed the journey to continue in mutual musical appreciation. 'Perhaps tonight will be a good night after all' mused Jake. Earlier in the evening he had contemplated cancelling on Sarah as his initial determination to get wasted had waned and overtaken by lethargy. His friend Jim had contacted Jake via text to inform him he would meet them both out this evening too, so with the prospect of letting two people down if, he decided to 'sack up' and go out.

As the taxi drove down Hainton Avenue, his mood soured. Jake glared out of the window and seeing the endless second-hand/ pawn shops, the 'we buy gold' type stores and payday lenders that spoke volumes about the town, he had pangs of regret about his actions at work. He lamented the days when such irritations didn't cause him to erupt in flashes of juvenile temper and longed for a way to control it. He blamed *her* and then realised he wasn't sure who he meant when he emphasised the word *her*. It dawned on him that thinking about these things, specifically the identity of *her*, wasn't helping his mood he tried to things about something, anything else.

As ever the case with Grimsby, distraction wasn't far away, but rarely positive as he spotted a group of shaved heads and tracksuits, each right leg tucked into the sock with nary a bike in sight, berating and spitting at a middle aged woman carrying her shopping. He tried not to stare, but the woman whilst annoyed, seemed to take it in her stride as if it was something she had just got used to. He wanted to destroy the tracksuits because he viewed them as a blight with no redeeming features, but he also wanted to shake the woman for being so passive, for letting them win.

The taxi drove past the Barge, shaking Jake from his anger. He looked outside at the benches and canopies that made up the beer garden and found no-one. It was early evening however, and mid-February. Years previously, at this time on a Friday evening, there would be many people outside the pub, but more and more revellers opted to come out later and later. Some choosing to drink beforehand to save money, others because it wasn't 'busy' enough for them yet. Jake grew incensed by the latter category, the type of person who couldn't enjoy themselves unless surrounded by people, regardless of whether they knew them. He saw it as a weakness of character; people who constantly craved validation. Social media extolled this sort of thing as a virtue and Jake feared it had become an epidemic.

As the taxi pulled up outside the Matrix club, he paid and thanked the driver. Then realised despite the clean car and the excellent music, the last six minutes had made him grumpier than when he left the house. 'Shots to start with then,' he resolved to himself as walking down the cobbled alleyway that led to the Matrix entrance.

The Matrix and the Barge frequently battled each other in Jake's mind for his favourite rock venue in the town. Hardly stiff competition as the only other was Old Lloyds which he had stopped his visits to years before as the smoking ban and lack of a beer garden had caused a separation between fag and pint. Currently, he leaned more in favour of the Matrix, because his friend, Craig, had moved from being the landlord of the Barge, to the landlord of the Matrix and had a tendency to be friendlier towards the 'old crowd' of which he had now become an unwilling member.

The interior of the club was one of contrast. Dark green walls with light wood panelling made it look more like a café than a bar. A huge screen projection TV adorned the wall next to the entrance, originally intended by the first owners to show football matches, yet now used to show cartoons or the DVD of Step Brothers on repeat. Jake was glad of the lack of football as he viewed rock pubs as an oasis to get away from the excessive emphasis on that boring sport, particularly during times such as the world cup where he could go out for a drink somewhere without the looming threat of inevitable violence.

Scanning the bar, there were two women and literally no-one else. He cursed himself for still having the 90s mentality of meeting for nights out at seven-thirty. Jake was also fifteen minutes early, so knew there would be some time before Sarah and Jim showed. He ordered four Sambuca and a Vodka Red-Bull in an attempt to shake his ennui. Jake drank two shots before his order was complete and idly chatted to Craig for a few minutes, then finishing the other two and taking his 'sipping drink' outside for a cigarette.

Jake had quit smoking about seven months previously having discovered e-cigarettes which he used to replace them almost entirely. One thing he couldn't change is the craving for the real ones when 'on the piss', so he had decided to buy a pack of twenty on any nights out and bin any left over the next day. It was rare there were any left over for the next day. Jake wouldn't admit to himself or others, but this also increased the amount of times he'd chosen to go out drinking.

He stood in a canopied area outside the entrance doors. Also standing outside was a woman he didn't recognise, in her late twenties who he found pleasing to his eye. What he didn't find attractive was her attire. She wore a faded towelled dressing gown, sweater, covering her nightdress, thick black tights and dirty grey socks accompanied by her rain soiled pink slippers. Convinced this must be some a joke, he tried to make light of it.

-   Ha-ha. Are you on a hen night or something?
-   Nuh.

The woman's face screwed in distaste at him. Already feeling lightheaded from consuming his daily allowance of alcohol units in a two-minute period, and thus oblivious to her discomfort he continued.

- I mean, the get up. Is it fancy dress? A dare?
- I can wear what I like when I go out. Women don't dress to please men you know.

Jake at this point noticed that due to the cold February air, and despite of the layers, he could see the outline of her nipples.

- So it's a statement then? Throwing off the shackles of the patriarchy by not bothering to get dressed when leaving the house?

Sarcasm dripped from Jake's utterance which was picked-up by the woman.

- No, it's just none of your business.
- Well, you kind of made it my business when I asked a simple question and you implied that I was some kind of lecherous oppressor when I asked a reasonable question about your clothing, which I'm sure you will admit is not only unusual, but very impractical at this time of year.

Jake's friends Sarah and Jim arrived and he secretly relished the thought of having spectators for this increasingly heated confrontation. Simultaneously, as he pointed out the time of year, the woman glanced down to her breasts and realised what he'd noticed seconds earlier and glowered at him.

- Besides, I thought this was a Greebo pub where none of you care how anyone else is dressed, anyway.

Jake had always hated the word 'Greebo', a colloquialism used as a term of hatred by what the country universally referred to as 'chavs'. A pejorative term to describe people with long hair and leather jackets in the eighties and nineties, but had since changed to describe anyone who enjoyed rock music, or even had the nerve to drink in one of Jake's 'big three' pubs. He thought the fact that people used it so freely was an example of how some types of irrational hatred such as racism were largely no longer tolerated, cultural prejudices still seemed to be fine. He used this outrage to justify getting nasty with the woman. That and the fact he now had an audience.

- Firstly, you do not, I repeat NOT, call anyone a Greebo. It's a term of abuse used only by the terminally thick, a category of which you certainly seem to occupy. Secondly, whilst you aren't forced to speak to me or engage with me in any way, it is hardly being offensive when there are only two of us stood here and I try to start up a conversation. And I totally agree that women don't have to tart themselves up to please men, wearing dresses and make up and the like it is bullshit. But don't stand there and try to say to anyone, let alone me, that by doing less than the bare minimum required for leaving the house I-fuckin'-E getting dressed that you are making a statement about that, because you are not, the only statement you are making to ANYONE is how you simply can't be arsed and that the people you mix with aren't worth the effort to spend thirty seconds throwing on a pair of jeans and a t-shirt/ sweater combination. If you were wearing a superhero outfit or were dressed like a giant... erm... (Jake struggled to find a word in short notice and opted for the first thing to enter his head) goat, I would have remarked upon it because it was unusual, NOT because of gender politics!

Jake's diatribe earned a stifled chuckle from Sarah and derisive guffaws from Jim. He knew Jim also hated it when he saw anyone leaving the house in bedclothes and he would freely admit that the reason he was labouring on this issue rather than simply walking away was as much for his benefit too. Shocked by his outburst, the woman meekly tried to change tact.

- Is this how you get your kicks? By trying to ruin other people's nights out? I came out for a drink with my friends and you come and casually judge me and give me all this shit...
- I'm not giving you shit! I'm giving you a gift! Of perspective and logic. A gift of self-respect. You are stood

out here on your own for fucks sake! Your friends clearly don't really want to be seen with you, otherwise they would be out having a fag with you. I'm not ruining your night out, I'm IMPROVING it. You can easily go home, get dressed in clean clothes and be back out to enjoy your night without embarrassing yourself AND the people you care about. And I mean this in the sincerest way possible that this entire situation could have been avoided had you not been so defensive about it in the first place!

The woman almost shook with rage as her friends came to investigate the raised voices. She looked at them and curtly stated 'I'll be back in a bit!' and left the premises without even finishing her drink. Sarah and Jim both felt guilty for laughing, Sarah more than Jim, but both knew Jake was already in the bull-headed stage of being drunk and it was best to let it fizzle out rather than to challenge it. One of the woman's friends quizzed Jake.

- What did you say to her? Why has she gone home?
- She went home to get changed. I told her she was making you both look bad.
- That's not true!
- You're welcome!

Jake dismissively waved his hand and sauntered back inside, followed by Sarah and Jim who offered token apologetic gestures. Jim ordered a Desperado and a White Russian for Sarah.

He walked over to the jukebox where Jake was poking the touch screen keyboard.

- How long have you been here mate? And what prompted all that?
- About ten minutes now. Ten minutes and already 50% of the pub hate me. Could be a new record!

Jim shook his head laughing. But part of him feared the night could potentially have more 'damage control' than relaxed drinking. 'Fuck it', he thought, 'I'll let Sarah deal with it!' He raised the first of what would be many Desperados to his lips and nodded appreciatively to the strains of Biohazard that interrupted the previous quiet of the Matrix. Jake was beaming, but his eyes betrayed the fact that there was no happiness behind the smile. Something was wrong and Jim knew tomorrow, they would need to talk.

Chapter 4.

Jim awoke to what he suspected was his worst hangover ever. His beard matted in foul smelling drool; he could smell Sambuca oozing through his pores. As he tried to leave the relative discomfort of his bed, he realised his entire body ached. A few tentative steps later and he realised he would be sick. As he shuffled towards the toilet as fast as his wasted muscles would allow, his cheeks swelled and filled with vomit. Clasping his fingers to his mouth to stem the flow proved to have merely a colander type effect as his bile sprayed through the gaps in his fingers splattering his walls, paintings and carpet with puke.

He made it to the toilet and after emptying the contents of his stomach, he then spent ten minutes with painful dry-heaves, the strain of which caused blood vessels in his left eye to rupture. He surveyed the damage in the bathroom mirror and shivered at how ridiculous he felt he looked.

Jim succumbed to male pattern baldness in his early twenties, but in an act of defiance continued to grow his hair in a style many compared to Hulk Hogan. Combined with his large, bushy beard and rectangular wire-framed glasses, some referred to him as 'Dungeon Master', which offended him but strengthened his resolve to not change the way he looked as to not let people see that his bothered him. His thirties contributed to his weight gain, and this had risen to other taunts such as

'Comic Book Guy' and 'Professor Special Brew'. The severe hangover, not sated by the copious vomiting attacked his ego as well causing him to resolve to stop drinking and make some changes.

Jim groaned as he staggered back to his bedroom, stepping in a half-eaten pizza he'd discarded the previous evening. He recollected the night's events and then stopped himself as he didn't want to deal with any inevitable embarrassment at this point. He knew he needed to clean up his sick from the landing area, but that could wait. Today was a write off, and he was spending it in bed. He drank nearly a full litre of lemonade, kept in a large bottle by his bed for times such as this and curled up, after remembering to put his mobile phone on charge.

Nine hours later the screen flashed to light with the name 'Pete' showing on the screen. Jim ignored this as he did for the next three times it rang. He clicked his phone into silent mode, he rolled over to gain more fitful, restless sleep. The phone continued to ring un-noticed for two more hours.

Chapter 5.

The night continued with gusto at the Matrix club. Jake, Jim and Sarah had been joined by a group of other friends and posted up by the pool table in the corner. By piling coins on the side, they'd basically guaranteed that it would be their domain for the foreseeable future. Yet games passed slowly due to constant interruptions by players buying drinks, visiting the toilet or going out to smoke. Because of this, Jake's attention towards the games wandered, as he often tended to do when drinking, to every other distraction and person in the bar. He often found himself in social situations surrounded by friends, yet they still could not hold his attention. He reasoned it may be a case of mild ADHD, or a simple side effect of the booze.

On this occasion, his attention focussed firmly on his friend Steve, a local dealer that provided him with cocaine and amphetamine on the rare occasions he desired it. He'd earlier surreptitiously texted the agreed code 'R U Coming 2 Matrix', the use of the hated text abbreviations as a signal it wasn't a social request. Steve arrived and motioned at Jake to go for a cigarette.

Steve was what many referred to as a 'gentleman dealer'. He only sold to his social circle, which widened due to the nature of his trade. His ever smiling face, which seemed to never age, was framed by a cascade of brown shoulder-length curly hair, often billowing out from beneath a cap. He never offered credit as he wasn't the type to commit, or even threaten, acts of violence. Steve's demeanour was amiable, and he was aware that drawing negative attention to himself would be a bad idea, so he remained chatty with landlords and doormen, winning them over with his easy-going charm. His caution paid dividends, and he'd been dealing ecstasy, cocaine and amphetamine for well over seven years. He never entered nightclubs that required any kind of search and always bought drinks in the places he frequented. His nights of business were Friday and Saturday nights, first frequenting the few pubs that his peer group attended; to sell to the people wanting to bolster their evening. He usually stayed awake until around seven in in the morning, to sell to those who wanted to extend their evening further. Because of this he remained careful about what he drank as he needed to be driving, so he drank no more than two alcoholic beverages. Also, he touched none of his wares and made a nice profit with no need to cut the goods any further. He also avoided any suspicious looking handovers on the premises of any venue since CCTV was rife in the area.

It was this caution that irritated Jake at that moment. Whilst smoking outside the pub, Steve handed over his mobile phone with a cat video playing on YouTube. His phone case folded back behind itself, allowing him to slip a gramme of cocaine into the case and the phone and the package to slide into the recipients hand as he passed it over. To the CCTV, it looked like a person sharing a stupid video on his phone, the worst outcome being if anyone saw tapes of him frequently, Steve would look like the type of idiot obsessed with cat videos. Although irked, Jake knew the routine well and slipped the fifty pounds into the back part of the phone as he handed it back.

The transaction complete, Steve drained his drink and set off to secure the rest of his evenings business and Jake returned to the bar for a further two shots and another Vodka Red-Bull. He noticed his group of friends dissipated to different areas of the bar. Sarah waited but now engaged in conversation with a boorish thug known to Jake as 'Scrobbo'. Sarah was smiling and laughing, but he could tell she seemed uncomfortable by her body language. She shifted position when reaching for a drink and looked cornered. Her eyes darted around for an escape route, but Scrobbo placed his sizable tracksuit wearing frame in her way.

Jake fired back his two shots in rapid fashion and then cursed himself for doing so, as they would be a legitimate reason to go to interrupt the conversation, so he ordered two more. Jake was intimidated by Scrobbo's size and propensity towards savage beatings, so he tried to envision a way to 'rescue' Sarah without raising the ire of the brutish chav. His drunken mind came up with a plan, of which he was later ashamed, but at the time he considered genius. He moved his left foot inwards and awkwardly lurched towards Sarah and Scrobbo.

-    Sarah! I gots your drink, but I spillded some of it!

Jake spoke much louder than he needed to in his best impersonation of how he imagined a mentally handicapped person may sound, he made awkward movements with his head to further stress the 'character' he tried to convey. Sarah stifled a giggle and immediately felt guilty for doing so. What Jake did was horrible, yet she remained glad for the interruption as the guy continued to insist she leave with him, despite her making the point she came out with her friends. She hated this kind of intrusion into her personal space and grew further incensed by the fact that because she'd politely laughed at his lame attempts at jokes, he'd assumed she wanted to sleep with him. Jake was being horrifically offensive, but the look of confusion that crept onto the guys face seemed priceless so she played along.

- Awww! Thanks Jakey! He is such a darl!
- I'm sorry I interump... interrumpted you talking Sarah!
- This guy was just saying he's having a party, Jake
- A party? Can I come? What's your name? My name is Jake!

Sarah feared Jake's performance was going overboard. It occurred to her it was becoming obvious that he took the piss. Scrobbo hadn't picked up on this, and his forehead crumpled on his close-cropped head as he tried to make sense of the situation. His first reaction to the new presence was to menace and intimidate, but with his current suspended sentence he needed to take it easy and everyone frowned upon 'leathering a spastic'. He was convinced he'd seen the person before and that he wasn't disabled, but couldn't be 100% sure. He decided discretion to be the better part of valour, although he would not have phrased it in that way and took his leave.

- Yeah. I'm Derek. I gotta go.

Scrobbo, now identified as Derek, a decidedly less threatening name, stormed away quickly. As he finished his drink from the other side of the bar, he glowered in Jake and Sarah's direction for a short time. Jake had noticed this and kept up his act for much longer than he originally intended fearing retribution if he didn't. Derek finished his drink and left the Matrix to go to a pub with 'less weirdos'. As Scrobbo/Derek left, Jake burst out laughing and turned to Sarah.

- Fucking moron. I can't believe he bought that!
- Why did you do that?

Sarah giggled, but genuinely wanted to know.

- I could see you getting bothered by him so I did the only thing I could think of. If I'd have gone up and butted in, he would have kicked off, probably smashing my face in. Then he would have still hung around you, twats like that reckon women get all wet for hard men. If I'd have told him to leave you alone, he would have DEFINITELY battered me, and I heard he stabbed a guy with a screwdriver a bit back. So the solution, other than leaving you to it, was to pretend to be retarded.

- Handicapped. But anyway, thanks. He scared me. I thought he was going to basically drag me away with him just because I gave him the time of day.
- Haha, you know my rule; if it wears a tracksuit, don't communicate with it!

Sarah wasn't happy that Jake made light of her fears, but still relieved to be out of the situation. Jake was already contemplating something else, however. The gramme of coke he had in his pocket called to him and the toilets in the Matrix were not fit for the purpose, having no ledge in the cubicle to make necessary preparations on.

- We off to the Barge then? I said we would meet Brian

This was a lie. Jake was aware that Brian would more than likely be there at some point, but he didn't want to let anyone else know about his coke, fearing they would want some too. 'Generosity goes out of the window when it comes to coke' he mused. Sarah agreed to depart and they set about alerting the rest of their friends they were leaving.

From a distance, Derek saw them leaving the Matrix and fury made him tense. He saw Jake animated and laughing with Sarah, who he liked and remained convinced it to be mutual. 'He'll get his' he sneered to himself menacingly.

Chapter 6.

Pete tried to contact Jim all the previous day and grew frustrated and aggravated that not only had he not answered his calls but also failed to return them. He tried to contact Jake the previous day as a simple confirmation they would both be visiting their parents, who returned from holiday. However, the repeated message that the phone was not available rang internal alarm bells for him. Initially he put it down to a network problem, but this carried on all day and with no activity on Facebook or any other social media apps Jake used, his panic grew.

He drove to Jake's flat and also received no response when pressing the buzzer. The next logical step in his mind was that Jake either crashed at Jim's place or got lucky and stayed with a woman, the latter option less feasible than it would have been ten years prior. There was an hour before they both were supposed to be at their parent's house and Jake wasn't the person to miss out on a free lunch without good reason.

Pete knocked loudly on Jim's door. After a minute, he saw the dishevelled figure of Jim clad in a fawn dressing gown, not dissimilar to the type worn by Jeff Bridges in The Big Lebowski. In other circumstances, he would have found Jim's laboured movements and obvious discomfort amusing, but not today.

- 	Pete? What's up?

Jim stood puzzled by Pete's appearance at his doorstep, although they were friendly, he'd never dropped by for a visit unless for some pre-arranged gathering.

- I've been trying to ring, and you didn't answer! I'm looking for Jake. His phone's switched off or something and we're supposed to be at our folks for dinner in an hour. Did he crash here?

- I'm sorry mate, I've literally been in bed since Friday night. I'm balls deep in two day hangover and had my phone on silent. He hasn't been here, no. Is everything all right?

- I dunno. Just not heard from him since Friday. Probably being a selfish cunt and just hasn't got in touch. Not like him to ever have his phone switched off though. I'm hoping to get a call five minutes before we're supposed to be there saying 'where are you? But he isn't at home right now either, or if he is, he isn't answering the buzzer.

Jim echoed Pete's concern. Jake would usually be the first to complain about people not returning calls or messages and would often inconvenience himself to answer a call to further illustrate his own point. Despite not knowing Jake's whereabouts, Jim suffered pangs of guilt, as if he'd done something wrong and desperately tried to offer some explanation for where Jake might be.

- I honestly couldn't tell you, I came home at about half two whilst Jake windmilled his arms and head across the dance-floor.

They both chuckled at the image they'd both seen on many occasions

- Have you tried Sarah? I saw them getting a bit friendly early on and it is possible he might have conned his way into her pants?
- All right, cheers. I'll check with her then. Fanny definitely is something he might turn his phone off for. Laters
- Later mate.

Jim closed the door and decided that after over twenty-four hours in bed, perhaps it was time to get up and clean up the puke he'd left on the landing yesterday. Pete turned and drove away, cursing himself for his absent-mindedness in not asking for Sarah's number. He knew Sarah to talk to when they went out, but never contacted her himself as he'd never needed a reason to. Jake befriended her when he worked for the DWP, unlike Jim, who became friends with Jake many years before that. Pete also had no idea where Sarah lived either and contemplated returning to Jim. He decided to let Jim be and contact her via Facebook and hoped that she checked it regularly.

About twenty minutes passed and Sarah replied to his message;

- Hiya! No not seen him since Friday. He came back here for a bit and left quite quickly. Let me know if you find him, he hasn't been in touch with me either xox

Pete swore quietly as anxiety took control of his mind and body. Pulling over and breathing heavily, he tried to take control of his racing thoughts and decide what to do. He wanted to ask his parents, but also didn't want to tell them his brother was missing. He felt alone and wanted to be angry at Jake for his selfishness, but something gnawed at his brain telling him this wouldn't be the case.

Realisation dawned that he needed to contact the police and by doing so he would need to tell his parents too. He couldn't imagine that anyone could have that conversation without causing more upset and alarm than necessary, and if that person existed, it certainly wasn't him. He left it until the last minute, reasoning that until Jake didn't show for dinner, it didn't mean he was missing—yet.

Chapter 7.

Jake, Jim and Sarah, accompanied by another four of their friends, Baz, Cash, Becky and her partner Scott all walked the short distance across Grimsby's town centre to the Barge. The journey usually took about four minutes on a normal day, but with a group of people in various degrees of alcoholic refreshment, this journey lasted for almost twenty minutes, causing aggravation to some.

As they crossed the bus station area of Grimsby towards the familiar surroundings of The Barge, Jake marvelled at how even after almost twenty years, it always remained a welcome sight. The Barge was as its name described. An almost floating pub dedicated to Rock and Metal fans in the area. It had been different colours on the outside over the years and if pressed, many would not be able to tell you if it currently was painted red or blue.

Outside stood an old concrete feeding trough with an inscription on it. This used to be used as an ashtray by patrons until the council filled it with soil and put in some plants, making it look more appealing and denying vagrants a place to piss. The block paved area outside had a chain fence surrounding it, designating the beer garden area. Contained within lay numerous picnic tables, some surrounded by partitions that supported canopies for shelter. Years previous, before the smoking ban, these tables were only out during the months of April through to October, but necessity meant that the seating area remained when people were no longer able to smoke inside.

Jake told his friends to order drinks and he would join them after smoking a cigarette. As he was the only one out there, he soon found himself lost in thought. He leaned on the railings outside and gazed into the filthy waters of the Freshney River. In his twenties, he used to enjoy being stood out here in the summer and would often enthuse to others that on a hot night, the combination of the lighting and the summer breeze to be one of the greatest free joys in life. Now, being a cold February night, these days seemed so far away.

He remembered the times in his teens and early twenties when he and all manner of people would congregate here after all the pubs and clubs had closed, to eat kebabs, pizzas and generally try to ride the high that the evening had generated. Often there would still be people there chatting until dawn and beyond, sobering up together after an evening of getting drunk at the same pace.

He missed those times as he considered himself a 'part' of something. The nineties brought the rise to a lot of variety in the Rock sub-culture; Grunge, Crusties, Indie Kids and Nu-Metallers as well as the old established groups as Glammys, Thrashers and Goths. During this time all seemed to inter-mingle and get on, something that carried on well into the early 2000s. Many new lifelong friendships formed over this time, some of whom came out with him that night. Every new face used to be a potential addition to the social circle. Now it seemed that any new face was a threat, a malevolent presence that hadn't voiced its distaste for him yet. Consequently, Jake spent most of his time on the defensive and tended to attack first, always verbally. These actions happened often enough to further separate him from those times.

As he wistfully reminisced about days gone by, isolation slowly grew in his mind. He'd come out with a group of close friends, a bond forged over almost a decade with some, more with others. Yet he thought he stood alone and could not explain why. He knew the evening was going to be the same as most evenings he'd enjoyed over the past few years; a few more drinks in The Barge and inevitably going into Gulliver's nightclub, the only 'proper' nightclub left in Grimsby. He tried to reason that this loneliness he experienced to probably be part of getting older– not being able to change with the times and not understanding why people started to enjoy what they did. He also reasoned there was more to it than that, younger people he had interacted with seemed to lack any self-awareness and unable to grasp the concept of irony unless shown in meme form. The obsession with communicating via text in SMS messages, Facebook and worse still, Twitter meant that offence often was easily taken as those formats contained no visual or vocal cues to pick up on. The ability to block people they disagree with meant that everyone perpetually lived in a closed ideology echo chamber never considering any other points of view or even facts that ever changed their outlook. Jake predicted that this would further hold back any societal progression, and this notion caused feelings of hopelessness and impotence that he could barely stand.

He tried to focus his thoughts again on happier memories, but this became fruitless since for every aspect of his life that he had a fondness for, there had been a reason it ended that he thought beyond his control. He wanted desperately to prove that he somehow still mattered and remained relevant in the world and found himself quietly crying into the murky water. Angry at himself for 'being such a fanny' he wiped his eyes and strode towards the pub entrance. The cocaine in his pocket called to him; it was a time machine back to the invincibility he felt during his formative years. He knew it to be temporary, but he figured that 'tomorrow would deal with itself'.

Chapter 8.

- It's been what nine? Ten months? I love you, but you have to do this for your own sanity.

Natasha pleaded with her long-term boyfriend Pete. She'd organised an event at the Matrix Club as a remembrance service as sorts for Jake. Arguments became more frequent on this topic as she tried various tactics to make him accept his brother wasn't, or was unlikely, to be coming back. As he hadn't been declared legally dead, no funeral service had been held, so she strongly believed this would help Pete overcome his obsession with finding him. Or at least reduce his nightly searches. The searches resulting in them barely spending any time with each other. The lonely nights making her consider leaving him, despite how callous that course of action would make her seem to others. Gently she continued to press.

- I've created an event on Facebook, and I've invited as many people as I have on my friends list that knew him, you need to invite the rest.
- What's the fucking point! It's not going to make me any less determined to find him! Or find out what happened!
- It's not about that Pete, it's for all of you to get together and y'know, share your pain or whatever. A small element of closure at least. Even if it doesn't help, it can't hurt or make things any worse!

- Closure for what? Police gave up, friends have given up, shit. Our own parents have given up! I'm the only one looking out for him anymore!
- They've accepted it. Accepted the most likely scenario. We've had this conversation, or at least a variation a thousand times. It is also a little while away yet, you can still look. You need to do this, if not for yourself, but for me. For us. I don't see you anymore...
- You see me every fucking day!
- That's not what I mean. We only speak to each other in passing. We don't spend time together like we used to, I'm more like a lodger in your bed than a girlfriend. I need to know you still want to be with me, no matter what happens. It's a horrible situation and I've stood by you and I need to at least acknowledge that you appreciate that.

Pete stopped himself from blurting out she never liked Jake. Her words, her tone made sense, and he didn't want to lose her as well as his brother. It was true they never got on. Natasha spent her early life in Capetown, South Africa and sported a slight accent. She was a tall, thin woman and was sensitive about her nose, which she considered too big and often upset by Jake constantly referring to her as 'Marabou Stork'. When Pete confronted him about this on a night out, he insisted it wasn't about her nose, because she was thin and from South Africa, it had something to do with a book by some Welsh bloke who wrote Trainspotting. Jake also explained the same night he always kept her at a small distance. Jake did this because if she ever did anything to hurt Pete, he would never hold any qualms on taking his side regardless of who was right or wrong. Jake also stated that after his own shitty experiences with girlfriends, he distrusted her, because of coincidental similarities, which he was aware were irrational, but made him suspicious anyway.

- Fine. I'll do it. Don't expect me to stop looking though.
- I don't. Thank you, it really does mean a lot. You don't have to stop, but maybe take a couple of nights off? I can see exactly what you mean, but after so many months, is it likely you will bump into him at any point? Whatever happens, I'm there, but you can't stop living your own life. If the worst has happened, do you reckon he would want that for you?

Again, Pete acknowledged that she was making sense to him. In truth, every time she'd made the point previously he'd agreed in principal, but he was unable to put it into words. He conceded it was time to try to at least balance things out a little.

- Ok. Ok. I just... still miss him. I dunno what to do and this is like... I'm doing something, rather than nothing.
- That's just it love, there isn't anything you can do now. It doesn't mean you have given up hope to live your life, it doesn't mean you don't care. It doesn't mean that your

family and his friends don't care. It's a dreadful thing to happen to anyone and if it is any consolation, I agree with you; I don't think he has done it to himself. He would tell everyone, probably in the most public way possible. Whatever has happened will come out and if he is somewhere around, then he will get found. No-one can completely disappear. Just wait. And hope.

Pete stood up and paced awkwardly back and forth. His jaw quivered and his eyes burned with tears he tried desperately to prevent from coming. As he clenched his teeth and dug his nails into his palms and tried to psych himself into anger over all other emotions, Natasha crossed the room and embraced him and the floodgates opened. He collapsed into her arms sobbing heavily. Months of repressing his feelings replacing them with confrontation, rage and accusations seemed to burst a psychological dam in an instant.

He and Natasha didn't speak for close to an hour and just held each other on their couch, fits of crying ebbed and flowed from both. Her because she hated to watch Pete like this, it hurt her to think of him this broken and imagined how she would be if Pete were to also disappear. She cried as she thought about how all of his family had probably done the same many times over the past few months, the family she also viewed as her own, that welcomed her in. Also she wept tears of relief because he'd finally let go of his stubbornness to move on and mourn, rather than search. Pete was crying for one sole reason. His emotional logic was dissipating, and he knew without a shadow of a doubt that Jake was gone and he would never see him again.

Chapter 9.

The coke burned Jake's sinuses after he'd taken a brief sojourn into the cramped confines of the Barge's lone toilet cubicle for a solitary 'toot'. The seat looked caked in light-brown vomit and he remained careful not to brush against the wall as he feared their stains to be smeared-on shit. He'd been informed by Craig, in the past, non-patrons would go in there and do a 'dirty protest' after seeing the place wasn't the den of debauchery they'd perceived it to be.

Cocaine was a drug that seemed to suit Jake perfectly. As a youth, he'd smoked cannabis, the resin form being popular at the time, and more often than not, done it to excess and found himself unable to move, head spinning and getting sick– or 'pulling a whitey'. As a person, he hated being slowed down and loved to talk, and the cocaine brought that side of him out in spades. He didn't do this often, reasoning because he enjoyed it so much, it would probably a bad idea to do it often as he was prone to addiction and overdoing it. Thankfully for him, it also stayed out of his price range to do it on the regular, so he saved it for times when he was particularly down.

As he left the toilets, his eyes darted around the pub for familiar faces, the long single room of the Barge making this easy. He spotted Jim and the crowd and headed over. As they drank and chatted, three women approached, one making a show of being held back by the others.

- Leave it Sophie, just enjoy your night.
- I'm OK, I just want to say my piece.

The woman, identified as Sophie stared confrontationally at Jake.

- This better for you? Are you happy now?

Bemused, Jake looked her up and down lecherously, much to the chagrin of the women. He admired the sheen to her bare legs, reddened by the exposure to the cold February air, her heels accentuating her calves in a way he liked and her tight black dress clung to her curvy, yet slender frame. His gaze turned up to her face, with expertly applied make up, causing her blue eyes to sparkle in contrast with her black hair cascading over her bare shoulders. He wasn't sure why she was angry at him, having forgotten their exchange from earlier.

- I'd buy that for a dollar.

Jim smirked at their mutual in-joke, but this seemed to infuriate Sophie further. She ignored her friends' pleas and continued to press.

- All you have to say? After giving me all that shit earlier?
- That was weeks ago, motherfucker

Sarah, Jim and the rest of their friends laughed at Jake's reference to Dave Chappelle. Jake soon remembered who Sophie was, the woman from the Matrix earlier he'd berated for wearing her bedclothes to the pub. She didn't get his reference at all and was perplexed why the others found it so funny.

- You're a piece of work. Thing is, when I saw you earlier, I quite fancied you until you opened your mouth. This is what you missed out on. Hope you are happy.
- Whoah. Whoah. Whoah there. Don't talk shit. I'm overweight, I'm older than you. There is no way in hell you fancied me, this is as pathetic as when a five-year-old says they will share their sweets to get back at someone for not doing what they want. And let's not forget, I saw what I missed out on already, you were dressed as you would be first thing in the morning. And what does this prove exactly? You said women don't have to tart themselves up to please men, yet here you are doing the OPPOSITE of what you said earlier. It's also worth noting, now you are dressed, your friends are actually stood by your side.

Sophie's friends cast him a venomous glance, but remained quiet. Jake continued uninterrupted.

- Fact is, the reason I talked to you in the first place was because I thought you looked attractive. I just can't stand people nowadays seem too lazy to even throw on a pair of jeans before leaving the house and I'd hoped you were doing it for a laugh rather than being one of those people. Don't forget, you were hostile first, calling me a Greebo and shit, you aren't as good at verbal jousting as I am. Don't be mad, few are.

Noticing the anger in her eyes, Jake softened his tone. He'd been in similar situations many times before, where a woman grew livid with him and he'd turned the situation around to the point where they'd forgiven him and frequently, ended up sleeping with him. This, of course, was in his twenties and his body was much slimmer. Despite thriving on being offensive, Jake hated to cause offence and viewed himself as merely 'cheeky' rather than malevolent.

- Seriously, despite how I made the point, don't you actually feel better? When I spoke to you earlier, you were defensive and stand-offish. Now you come up all guns blazing, full of confidence, with your friends. You haven't done this to please me, or any other man, I totally get it; you have done it for yourself. You didn't know you would run into me again.
- I hoped I would so I can tell you what a dick you are
- I know I'm a dick. I make a point out of it. This isn't a revelation. We can carry on bitching at each other and you will end up walking away angrier than you were before and I will forget about it a few minutes later

because I'm already leathered. You have made your point, you look stunning, you're are a pretty woman, anyway. If all it took was someone being a bit of an arsehole to you to shake you out of whatever funk you were in before, then how can that be a bad thing?

Despite herself, Sophie blushed at his effortless flattery. She saw his point, even warming to him. Sarah looked on with a pang of jealousy that shocked her. 'She's going to fuck him,' she snapped in her mind, with a bitterness that came as a further surprise. Sophie's friends both were relieved their friend returned fully dressed, their support being token rather than in full agreement. Jake continued in a placatory manner.

- I can see I'm making sense and for what it is worth, I'm sorry to upset you. But it was clearly for the greater good you know?
- I don't know. I think I've betrayed myself just to prove a point now.
- But you haven't! Betrayed yourself I mean. You don't NEED to prove a point to anyone, least of all me. All of this started by you trying to prove a point, which was muddled and honestly, not very well thought out. Look, let's have a drink and forget about it all.

Sarah turned and motioned for a cigarette to the others. There were no takers, so she left to go outside, as she turned she glanced at Jake and Sophie, who now stood close together at the bar, Sophie throwing her head back and laughing at something he said. Again, Sarah's envy rose and she couldn't explain why. She and Jake had been mates for a few years now and there'd been no suggestion of anything other than friendship between them. She suspected when she met him he wanted something to happen, but he hadn't pushed the situation and caused any awkwardness, because she hadn't considered him as a partner, sexual or romantic. Yet after this evening, his 'rescue' from the big, scary guy combined with her very real want for him to be happy triggered something inside. She reasoned the same things that eliminated him from being a potential boyfriend in the past still applied; he was pretty shiftless, with no idea what he wanted from life or work, etc. He obviously didn't care about the work he had. He seemed flaky and quick to anger at work. She contemplated the possibility she could change those things about him, to give him a reason to care about life again.

Sarah realised she'd spent more time with Jake than any other guy and the thought of being without him upset her. Did she love him? She certainly loved being around him, but still couldn't picture being intimate with him. As if on cue, Jake appeared beside her lighting a cigarette, eyes frantic and wide.

- Fucking smoking ban. It's all right in the summer, quite glad of it, everyone comes out to join you, but not when it's freezing like this.

Sarah smiled.

- At least you came to join me.
- Course I did, I wouldn't leave you stood out here on your own.
- What about that lass? You seemed to be getting cosy with her?
- Haha. Maybe ten years ago. I can't be bothered with the drama. You end up banging someone you've already had a row with, it never usually ends well.
- Perhaps she would be different? Not everyone is the same after all.

Sarah cursed herself. Why was she trying to talk him into it? Was it because she wanted reassurance he preferred to be here with her? 'Am I that needy?' she thought to herself.

- I was nice to her, sort of, in the end. But that doesn't change the fact she came to the pub in her dressing gown and slippers. She's a moron. Don't get involved with morons. Plus, I have more of a laugh with you, my bottom bitch.
- Damn right I'm your bottom bitch!

Sarah loved the in-joke that over time, developed between them. If anyone else referred to her as a bottom bitch, she would have been offended. It stemmed from a few Christmas periods ago, when she'd bought Jake a giant pimp hat with a feather in as a joke and he wore it all evening and pretended to be a pimp all night, calling all women in his vicinity 'hoes' much to their chagrin, but made her laugh until tears sprang from her eyes. He then proclaimed her to be his 'bottom bitch' and she would 'make daddy the most money'. Like many times, Jake often went too far when he drank, but providing you were with him, it always seemed hilarious. Thinking about this, how much fun she'd over the years, she decided to kiss him. She reached over to touch his arm to bring him in for a hug, to make it seem natural, like he'd initiated it, but his attention was already elsewhere.

- ROGER! YOU FUCKING BELLEND!

Jake screamed at a man Sarah correctly assumed to be Roger across the bus station, who meekly waved in response, sober and embarrassed by the unwanted attention.

- YOU OFF TO GULLIES LATER?
- Nah! Work.
- NO WORRIES MATE! SEE YOU ROUND!

Roger scurried away, face red. Jake then discarded his finished cigarette into the river and clapped his hands together with a loud slap.

- Right then! Shots!

Sarah nodded and forced a smile. He hadn't noticed her intent, but she felt mildly humiliated anyway, as if he'd somehow rejected her. For them to be alone, in the quiet again wouldn't be likely for the rest of the evening. The moment passed and Jake hadn't been aware there was a moment to be had.

Chapter 10.

Two weeks after Jake disappeared, Sarah was inconsolable. What started out as friendship had grown stronger as a line from some 80s track sang on the radio in the background. The aptness of the lyric brought on a fresh wave of tears, circumstances that became more commonplace the longer he'd been gone.

After the last time they'd seen each other, they'd forgone the usual jaunt to Gulliver's nightclub and gone back to her place. He'd seemed so tender and loving, she'd gone in for a hug and he squeezed her tight and then they kissed deeply, tongues probing each other's mouths with an urgency like it was their last night together on earth. She'd been with many guys, including previous relationships, where this type of situation had become simply a case of perfunctory foreplay in a rush to male climax. Jake had been different though, he didn't seem to be in any rush at all and seemed a lot more sober than their several hours drinking allowed. Their clothes were slowly shed and his hands stroked and teased her in all the places she enjoyed. It was as if she'd given him a map and directions to every single one of her erogenous zones, yet he seemed instinctive and cared as much about her pleasure as his own.

In a post coitus daze, he'd held her for a long time and she noticed a sadness in his eyes that spread empathetically to her. She'd considered the evening to be the beginning of a relationship, despite her misgivings, she now wanted. She asked what was wrong, and he'd replied nothing, smiled and kissed her again. Now with hindsight, she felt guilty because she hadn't pressed the issue, not noticing his rare silence to indicate something worse. Her guilt doubled because of how angry she got initially because he hadn't called her. Every day that passed until she'd found out he'd gone missing, she called him all the spiteful names she could remember, considering herself to be humiliated and used. With him gone, this anger became re-directed towards herself.

Sarah remained convinced Jake took his own life, yet was unable to voice this to anyone who close to him as they still hoped he would be found safe and alive, with tales of some misadventure gone awry. As a result, she'd mourned him alone. She wanted informing why he'd abandoned everyone without so much as a note and fantasised possibilities that may have made him think life was worth living if he'd only talked to her. Sarah also wished her perception was wrong and others to be right. She wanted to see him again with a gnawing desperation, so joined in search efforts she inwardly considered being futile. Sarah couldn't remember a time in her life she wanted to be wrong as much as she did now.

Chapter 11.

Sarah, Jim and Jake realising the night was towards its end, headed to Gulliver's nightclub. Situated less than a hundred metres away from the Barge, there wasn't much of a journey which explained why it remained the only nightclub left in Grimsby; convenience. Jake had never been enthralled by the place, but compared to the thumping dance music heavy clubs of the neighbouring town Cleethorpes, it seemed like heaven.

Gulliver's looked nothing like the way most people imagined nightclubs. A single small doorway let to some rickety stairs that took people up to the first floor location of the clubs interior. The walls painted a drab greyish-blue and the club itself was dark, close-to-black walls with crumbling mirrors framing the dance-floor. Back in the early nineties, when Jake had first ventured inside, the place was always full and when a rowdy song came on, he always feared the dance-floor would collapse due to its flimsiness. Yet the club had become a Grimsby institution, a part of most people's nights out at the end.

In the present, Gulliver's often seemed desolate. The smoking ban had hit Grimsby particularly hard with many pubs closing and changing hands multiple times. As a small venue, Jake figured that it was not a great deal less busy than it ever used to be, but that many people would smoke outside at any given time, freeing up a lot of space and making it seem emptier. Although on this evening, it was unusually busy, full of unfamiliar, younger faces that both Jake and Jim took an instant dislike to, simply by virtue of the fact that the people were younger and an old man jealousy took hold. Jake, fuelled by the remnants of the cocaine he bought earlier ranted to an agreeable Jim.

- Look at that fucker. Preening little tosspot. Gelled up quiff-having bell end. Hipsters piss me off, if they are not growing beards and spending their time solely defining themselves as 'beard have-rs,' they are wearing this skinny jean uniform for cunts. I know fashions always seem stupid to older people since time began, but for fucks sake, how can any of these twats think they look good?
- I know mate. And them pointy fucking shoes. That dickhead looks like how I imagine a pixie would.
- Yeah, it isn't just the guys though. The women, with those stupid messy beehives. Did it ever occur to them that Amy Winehouse wasn't a style icon, she was probably too fucked up to sort her hair out properly?
- Ha! Definitely would her though.

Jim nodded toward a young woman on the dance-floor lecherously. Jake looked her up and down as if a connoisseur of the female form and shook his head in a dismissive motion.

- Ergh god no. Not only does her hair appear like it could be the living quarters for a family of crows, but she clearly loves herself way too much. We've been stood here barely minutes and when she isn't looking at herself in the mirror, she is taking selfies. Unless your cock somehow managed to add a thousand likes on Instagram, she wouldn't touch it.
- My cock gets loads of likes on Instagram mate.

Sarah, offended by the exchange and its pure objectifying tones wanted to leave and hope the conversation played itself out. She often knew Jake liked to joke, playing the sexist pig role in an ironic manner, this time she wasn't sure whether he was joking around or being a genuine arsehole.

- I'm off to get the drinks in, you two staying here in Judgement Corner?

They both smirked at the nickname they gave to this spot in Gullivers next to the dance-floor. So called because people watched the others dancing with barely disguised contempt. This was partially true, but the real reason Jake and Jim favoured this spot was that it had an area to keep drinks relatively guarded from minesweepers, it was close to the dance-floor in case a song they wanted to slam about to came on and most importantly, they were fat and it had the only fan in the building. Jake handed Sarah ten pounds.

- Yeah, we're staying here, I'll pay for these. Desperado for Jim, my usual and whatever you are having. We're going to stand here and idly toy with the notion that two overweight, middle aged men would ever turn down the chance to sleep with a woman in her mid-twenties based on her hair style.
- Speak for yourself mate, I do all right.

Jake turned and stared Jim directly in the eyes with as blank an expression as he could muster at the time.

- Worst. Dungeon Master. Ever.
- Fuck you.

Sarah was relieved to see that whilst the tone of the conversation was dreadful, at least there was an element of playfulness rather than malice and turned to get the drinks. Jake's mood turned maudlin and began to consider for the second time that evening how the world had passed him by and he thought he had nothing to look forward to in life but to face one setback after another.

- In all seriousness dude, what the fuck are we doing? Why are we even in a nightclub at our age? Why are we stood ragging on younger people for the way they are dressed?

- Because they look like cunts mate.
- True, ha-ha, but we looked like cunts too back in the day. Jeans so baggy that they were basically piss flannels when we went into the toilets at Hollywood's. Wallet chains that came down lower than our knees we constantly tripped on. Limp Bizkit hoodies. I mean come on. Limp Bizkit? Why did we even listen to that shit, let alone paying to advertise the fact as well? I mean 'our day' has been and gone. We've got nothing left. We either stay doing what we're doing and look sadder and sadder doing it as the years go by, or we succumb to the drudgery and wait for death. Some look forward to retirement. I don't. It's when we have to pay the bill for all these years of excessive drinking, smoking and casual drug use. I'll be lucky to live to sixty-eight or whatever age these Tory wankers determine we will have to work until. If by some miracle I do, I will have breathing problems, heart problems and my liver would probably be shagged out.
- Mate, I didn't get a word of that. You're slurring.

Jake conceded that he'd had way too much to drink and his body could not keep up with his racing mind in both speech and movement. He contemplated trying to repeat his point, but couldn't remember where he began. Sarah came back over to them with their drinks plus a tray of cheap shots that Jake disliked, but drank anyway. Upon drinking his two shots, Jim, a notorious lightweight amongst his friends, wrestled with the urge to vomit for several minutes and won the battle temporarily whilst Sarah and Jake chatted. He decided now it was time to 'tap out' and head home.

- I'm done. I'm off home.
- Why?

Jake replied out of concern for both his friend's well-being and the nagging doubt he'd aggrieved him without realising.

- I've had to stop myself from spewing. If I have another drink, I won't be able to.
- Just drink water for a bit, you'll be fine.
- No I won't. I need to go to bed.
- Ok Fair one. I'll catch you soon yeah?
- Yeah. Laters.

Jake watched Jim depart from the club with a mild stagger. It occurred to him he'd lost the rest of the group at some point in the evening, but couldn't remember why or when they left. He looked out of the window of Gullivers onto the bus station/ taxi rank area to see if any of them were still about. He noticed Sophie furiously kissing a guy whilst waiting for a taxi and smiled. Sarah was also ready to leave, but not ready for the night to end. She often found Gullivers to be quite boring after the peak time when they played a mixture of classic rock songs such as Journey and RamJam. Now, finally alone with Jake, she thought about making a play for his affections again, but in an environment with less distraction.

- I'm bored. Shall we go?
- What!? Now you're pussying out too? There's over an hour left for Christ's sake!
- No, I mean, let's go have a few at mine and watch something. It's pretty boring here tonight and we know no one, anyway.
- Ok. Yeah, I guess you're right. Finish our drinks first though yeah? Not wasting them after paying these prices.

Jake thought about dragging the drink out and maybe talking Sarah into having another, to try to see the evening through to completion. He was unaware that Sarah had intentions of intimacy and saw it as an evening that had yet again failed to live up to expectation. He groaned loudly when The Killers–Mr Brightside was played by the DJ and realised the next hour to likely be full of 'indie crap' so quickly demolished his Vodka Red Bull and prompted Sarah to do the same. Sarah now mildly regretted her decision to leave as she fancied a dance, but was glad that she would get to be alone with Jake.

As they both walked back to her home, laughing and joking, they failed to spot Scrobbo, his night also ending at the same time, much further down the street behind them. It took several minutes for him to register their presence, but he recognised them and followed until they entered the door of Sarah's rented house.

Chapter 12.

- Pete? It's Jim
- Yeah? What's up mate?

Pete felt perplexed by the phone call. Jim rarely had a reason to contact him.

- Have you heard from Jake?
- No, he was out with you last night wasn't he?
- Yeah. Look, we had a long talk last night and I'm probably being stupid, but he said some stuff that is really bizarre as fuck, but he was so insistent it has kind of stuck with me, can we meet up for a coffee?
- Err, yeah. I'll be in town in an hour I guess.

Pete hung up the phone and tried to call Jake. The call went straight to voicemail. Concerned, Pete resolved to call in to Jakes' flat on the way to town.

Chapter 13.

Sarah made cups of tea for her and Jake as he sat in her room playing music videos on YouTube. She contemplated pouring them both vodka drinks, but reasoned that considering her plans, she didn't want him to be even more pissed than he already was. Her sudden change in how she saw him, from friend to a potential partner has intrigued her and she wanted to act on it and considered now to be the perfect time. She carried the two mugs of tea through to her spacious, yet sparsely furnished living room.

Jake beamed at her as he accepted his tea, then much to Sarah's disappointment, as soon as she sat down on the couch next to him, he sprang up and went to the bathroom. As the music on the current video died, she realised why he'd left the room abruptly as she listened to loud farts emanating from the toilet. She giggled, but her ardour had been dampened. It quickly returned as she remembered times in her own past when she'd done exactly the same thing. She took it as a positive sign he held deeper feelings for her too.

Jake returned, unaware that Sarah heard his arse-utterances and weakly tried to explain that he'd gone to 'wash the nightclub stamp off my hand' and explained that if you didn't do it on the night, it stayed for days afterwards as if to explain his 'longer than a piss' absence. Another music video began; Kansas–

Carry on My Wayward Son and distracted him from his rambling justifications.

- I love this one. Had it since I was about ten.
- Me too. Love it I mean. I only heard it when it was on Supernatural.

An awkward silence passed, with neither Jake nor Sarah being able to think of anything to say. Both sat and watched the grainy footage of the ugly musicians play in silence. Sarah took the initiative and started softly stroking the back of Jake's hand with her finger, whilst still staring at the TV screen. Jake smiled. He'd hoped this would happen for years and reciprocated clasping her hand into his. The innocuous gesture meant more to him than any sex he'd had in the past few years, as the gesture seemed intimate and a sign of genuine warmth. He pulled her closer and draped his arm around her and looked into her eyes, she leaned in to kiss and he rushed to meet her, faster than he'd intended, clacking teeth and butting heads as they probed each other's mouths.

Jake lowered her beneath him on the sofa and began crudely kneading her breasts. Sarah grimaced as her arm became trapped underneath and behind her and she feared it would break under both of their weight. She hooked her leg around Jake's and using all her strength flipped them over onto his back. However, the settee wasn't big enough for such a manoeuvre and he came crashing to the floor with her landing on top of him. He groaned and for a few seconds Sarah thought he'd prematurely ejaculated, but realised that he lay winded and struggling for air. Not knowing what to do she dismounted and rolled him onto his side asking 'are you ok?' every few seconds.

Jake was fine after he'd regained his breath and told Sarah so as she apologised and kissed his face. The hardwood floor hurt his elbows, so he stopped Sarah.

- Can we take this upstairs?
- I think we should

Sarah kissed him again and grabbed his hand, only pausing for a moment as she mentally noted that she hadn't left any dirty laundry on the floor, or worse still, her vibrator drawer open. Confident it wasn't the case, she bounded up the stairs with him in tow. She led him through the dark onto the bed and took off her shirt. She didn't switch on the lights as she was self-conscious about her body, whilst not dramatically overweight, she was ashamed of parts and proud of others. Jake was glad of the darkness, he despised seeing himself naked and didn't imagine that anyone else would want to. His eyes grew accustomed to the murk and saw a moonlight silhouette of Sarah wearing her bra looming over him. At that moment she looked to him as sexy as anything he'd ever seen and he grabbed her waist spinning her round onto her back on the bed. Jake kissed her for a few moments, he worked his lips down to her neck as he unclasped her bra with his right hand. So impressed was he upon achieving this he needed to make a point out of it.

- One handed bra unhook first attempt! Get in!

Sarah however was unimpressed and ignored the remark for fear of losing momentum. He roughly mashed her left breast with one hand, whilst kissing and licking the right. She was enjoying the sensation until he bit on her nipple. He mistook her pained gasps for those of pleasure and continued to focus on this until Sarah needed to grab his head and kiss him again.

As they rolled onto their sides, Jake reached his hand to between her legs and massaging her groin. His fingers missed her clitoral area by a good two inches and he merely rubbed her pubic bone. She wore jeans and helped him by guiding his hand under the belt line. Exasperatingly for her, he still didn't reach the right spot, so she unbuckled her jeans and threw them onto the floor, whilst he did the same. Whilst he did so, he pulled out a condom from his pocket and placed it on her bedside table. Sarah noticed that the drawer remained ajar and closed it.

- So it doesn't fall in

He then positioned himself between her legs and bent down to kiss her again and his erection swell against her pudenda and she ground against it. He paused and reached between her legs, finally his fingers exploring the sweet spot and she relaxed and became aroused again. This happened for about twenty seconds before Jake reached over for the condom and put it on in a hurry. Annoyed that the foreplay was seemingly and unsatisfactorily over, she then grew pleased when he'd rubbed the head of his cock against her clitoris. She helped guide him herself and was back in the moment again. He then slid himself into her, making her disappointed that the sex was being rushed.

His irregular thrusts made it impossible for Sarah to enjoy the sex. As soon as they achieved a rhythm, he would slow down, destroying it. He changed positions often, always when she started enjoying the one they were in. She forcefully span him onto his back, determined to get some enjoyment out of this tryst, planning on riding herself to climax. He grasped her buttocks and began quickly thrusting from underneath and combined with her own movements she rapidly chased an orgasm when he suddenly yelped and she felt his dick crumble inside her.

-   Arghh! Bent the fucker!
-   Sorry, got carried away. Let's carry on!
-   I can't. It got bent in half. It's happened before.

Sarah leaned in to kiss him again, stroking his thighs and trying to tease his flaccid penis back into life. After a few minutes she realised this wasn't happening and snapped angrily at Jake.

-   I'm off to the bathroom! Next time, take your t-shirt off!

Jake was dejected. He knew the sex was bad from her reaction and even if his cock hadn't been folded over into uselessness, he was close to faking a finish because he knew it would not happen. He'd broken his golden rule; don't fuck your friends and worse still, he'd fucked her badly whilst drunk and incapable. He lay back and hoped that when she said 'next time' she really meant it. The combination of drink and exertion made his eyelids heavy, and he lay back to doze.

Sarah regretted scolding Jake. They were both drunk, and the sex was awful. Whilst angry at him for his poor and selfish performance, she also thought she'd taken the wrong opportunity for this to happen and should have waited until she sobered up to see if she felt the same way before trying anything. Sarah hoped that they hadn't irreparably damaged their friendship, or possible future as a couple and resolved to forget about tonight and see what would happen in the coming week. In her anger, she'd stormed downstairs naked and now was bashful about re-entering her bedroom that way, so she wrapped a towel around herself before going back upstairs. She thought about just being on the bed with Jake and sleeping together, hopefully to show there to be no hard feelings.

As she walked into the bedroom, she saw Jake was not there and his clothes had gone. She assumed he'd left without saying a word.

- Fucking bastard!

Chapter 14.

Pete arrived at a locally run coffee shop, Riverhead Coffee, to meet Jim. Pete suffered a great deal of anxiety, partially because of the phone call he received by Jim, but also because there was no response as he knocked on the door to Jake's flat. It wasn't his preferred choice of meeting place as he wasn't much of a coffee drinker although at least he would be able to talk without the distraction of irritating Jazz music blaring through the speakers favoured by the chain coffee stores.

He walked to the upstairs seating area and noticed to his annoyance that Jim had not arrived yet. As he was five minutes late himself, this angered him even more considering the urgent nature of Jim when he called. He sat in the corner in one of the mismatched comfy chairs. The whole shop looked like it had relied on donated furniture for seating; no two seats were the same. It created a rustic, 'lived in' vibe that on any other occasion would have seemed relaxing.

Jim ambled up the stairs a few moments later with a caramel latte, or 'twatacinno' as Jake often referred to anything other than straight coffee ordered in these places. He sat next to Jim on another armchair in the corner and nodded a curt greeting. Pete had grown more impatient with every minute that Jim was not here and snapped angrily.

- You're fucking late. I'm all panicked and you've left me here stewing.
- Sorry mate, I was filling the car up on the way and there was a line.
- You could have done that afterwards! Ah forget it. Look, what is going on? I've been trying to ring Jake, and the phone isn't switched on and I called in on the way, no response. Is he OK?
- Sort of. This is really difficult to say, and it's pretty unbelievable. I didn't believe it, but Jake was stone cold sober when he told me and there was something in his eyes, like a desperation that convinced me.
- That's no kind of answer! What. The. Fuck. Is. Going. On!

Pete's uncharacteristic venom startled Jim. He knew this would be a difficult conversation to have, but would never have predicted any anger, let alone the commanding tone and a hint of violence that seemed to ooze from every deliberate, hissed word coming from Pete's mouth. He continued to explain, but in much more placatory tones.

- I'm not trying to be evasive or anything like that. Please understand that I'm struggling with this myself and I need you to listen. Jake needs you to listen. It's so far out there that I honestly don't know where to begin.
- Then just fucking well say it!

- Jake is trapped in the same night over and over again. Like Groundhog Day, but without the laughs.
- Fuck you, I'm going!

Pete rose sharply and was considering kicking Jim in his face. Jim rose also and grabbed Pete's arm and guided him back into his seat. Despite himself, Pete allowed this to happen.

- Like I said, this is unreal. I was a little pissed when he told me so that may have helped. I was sober by the end. We were talking for about two hours and he explained as much as he can to me.
- Exactly what did he say?
- Basically what I've just told you. In a nutshell; every time he goes to sleep, he wakes up back in a taxi ready to go out last night. He doesn't know how or why it is happening, he has no idea how to stop it, or what happens afterwards. Jake said he has told me before and that he has tried to tell you over the phone, because you were out with Natasha last night, so he couldn't get to see you to convince you. He guesses he is probably missing and from how it seems, he is right in that guess.
- Are you two trying to wind me up? This is bullshit that no-one would ever take seriously.
- No. Like I keep saying, this is hard to grasp for me too. We might be a pair of dicks, but do you reckon we would try to wind you up to this extreme?

- Jake would! And you pretty much go along with whatever he says, anyway!

- He wouldn't, not like this. He has never gone out of his way to worry you. He specifically told me to tell you like this, in person and not to let you think any different. You heard from him last night and saw him a few days ago yeah? He hasn't seen you or your parents in months. He is desperate to see you and has tried to get you to cancel your plans with Natasha once, but it never happens. Your folks get back from holiday on Sunday don't they?

- Yeah, so?

- So you will see them then. Sunday doesn't exist for him. He says it is like a prison sentence almost, with no visitation rights.

Pete's mind raced. He still considered walking out, knowing if it were a cruel prank, they wouldn't keep it up for long. Jake had played various jokes on him in the past and he remembered the worst when he still lived with his parents, they had gone away and when Jake was round, he had snuck upstairs and filled his waste paper bin with burnt tin foil and a burnt spoon, with the handle bent round underneath. When his parents returned, he told them he thought Pete was a heroin addict. Having found the items in the bin, his mother had freaked out, making Jake laugh until he cried. Pete had laughed too later on when Jake had explained that before this some tabloid had run a ridiculous guide on how to spot if your child was on drugs and that his parents had tried applying this to Pete. Regardless of the joke, Jake would never carry it on for any length of time. Pete decided to at least play along–at the worst Jake would turn up and laugh at him for almost believing it. Or possibly, he considered, that would be the best scenario.

- So what can we do?
- Very little, apart from be aware that he is ok, or at least alive. I've a few theories based on what he said, that what happens right now, might not happen again depending on what he does that night.
- So nothing?
- He said we need to do one more thing; we need to explain this to Scotch Terry. Jake reckons maybe he can help.

Chapter 15.

- Where to mate?

Jake was startled by the fact he found himself sat in the back of the plush taxi from the evening before. He remembered being in bed post coitus at Sarah's and concerned that somehow he'd blacked out or damaged his memory after the previous evening. A bizarre coincidence he'd taken the same taxi again, but wondered why he'd planned on an evening out again. He pulled his phone from his pocket in an attempt to piece together more information. As he did, the taxi driver repeated his query in a more impatient tone.

- C'mon mate, where you going?
- I… er…Matrix in town, please.
- No worries.

Jake checked the variety of message apps he used on his phone; text, WhatsApp and Facebook messenger. Seeing nothing new he remained baffled and then heard the opening chords of 'Slave to the Grind' simultaneously noticing the date on his phone. The first word that stood out: 'Friday'. He double checked other apps and also two news sites and they all said the same. 'Wow' he thought, 'I've dreamt a vivid dream whilst being awake'. He reasoned there to be no way that the evening took place based on the facts shown on which day it was and him not suffering a monstrous hangover. Hangovers were a price seldom paid in his twenties, but with interest now in his thirties for his frequent nights of excess. He considered what he'd experienced to be strange, but not unexplainable and that the similarity between the song playing in his dream and now could more than likely be a subconscious thing; he'd probably been in this taxi before and the driver likes Skid Row.

Whilst Jake was lost in thought, the taxi seemed to arrive quickly at the Matrix, with Jake barely observing the journey. He thanked and paid the taxi driver and started inside. He made his usual order and threw back the calming shots of sweet liquor. Jake opted for a cigarette whilst waiting for his friends to arrive. He was further alarmed to see Sophie, adorning the same dressing gown and slippers she'd worn in his 'dream'. He quickly turned away and smoked his cigarette in nervous silence. 'This is too bizarre for words' he wondered if his dream was the phenomenon known as 'prophetic dreaming', his panic giving way to possibilities for a talent he wasn't sure he possessed. He would definitely use it to play the lottery should the situation arise again. Jake engaged in his frequent fantasies of having no financial worries for his friends, family and self. He carefully planned his potential purchases, and this buoyed his mood somewhat. He barely realised Jim and Sarah had arrived.

- I think it's fucking finished mate!

Jim laughed and pointed to the cigarette which had burned down to the filter, yet Jake hadn't realised, still absent-mindedly puffing away on nothing. He flicked the cigarette at the wall and it landed perfectly still on a small shelf of brickwork. He grinned and thrust his fists in the air at the faux display of cigarette butt flicking 'skills'.

- Ninja skills! Let's get fucked!

Sarah, Jim and Jake made their way to the bar and idly chatted for a while. As more people entered the pub, Jake spotted Sophie sat in the corner, face burned into an angry scowl as her friends, although sat nearby, their distance was that of not wanting to be associated with her. Sophie's eyes threatened tears, but she seemed to be too angry to let them happen. After several minutes she seemed to realise that she was fighting a losing battle and made a sharp exit. Her friends barely acknowledged her leaving, and it took a while for them to register that she'd left her drink and had gone for good. Jake saw the shaking heads and shrugged shoulders that showed they were indifferent to this and remembered his aggressive exchange with her from the 'dream'. Hell, he was right! Whilst this was different to the way it happened in the dream, he still assumed he'd somehow predicted this. His thoughts went back to the imagined lottery millions he would gain through his newfound 'skill'.

As the group expanded with the arrival of their friends, they made their way over to the pool table area and the conversation turned into somewhat familiar territory for Jake again. He continued drinking, enjoying the company and had seemingly forgotten his bizarre stint as a seer, when he saw the close cropped simian head he knew as Scrobbo dragging his wiry, yet muscular frame behind it into the Matrix.

Chapter 16.

'Scotch' Terry wheezed as he lowered himself down onto his nicotine stained couch to flick through the channels to pass the time in what he considered being a worthless existence. In his youth, he'd been known as an intellectual young man, effortlessly gaining both his degree and master's degree in physics before moving from his native Glasgow to Bristol to study for his doctorate.

During his time in Bristol, he met and fell in love with Shelley, something he would profess that happened the moment he saw her curly brown hair and large brown eyes that lit up when she smiled. Terry overcame his usual shyness around the opposite sex and he'd struck up a conversation with her and was overjoyed to find that they'd much in common and that she was also a pleasure to talk to. More importantly, to him was that somehow she felt the same way, and he was thankful for everyday they spent together. The couple moved in with each other soon after into a grotty flat that neither seemed to mind, being so enamoured with each other.

Shelley studied on the final year of her degree, however and couldn't afford to stay in Bristol, having a job waiting for her back in her hometown of Grimsby. Terry decided that he would move there with her and put a hold on his doctorate for the time being until they were both in a comfortable financial position to move back. He assumed that being a well-educated person he would have no difficulty in finding a fairly well paid position temporarily to speed the process along.

Upon moving back to Grimsby, Shelley fell pregnant to Terry and whilst they both realised this would be a stumbling block for their future plans, they remained overjoyed at the prospect of raising a family together. Shelley's family supported them and had no problems with allowing Terry to stay with them in the parental home to help them save for their future together.

What Terry hadn't factored in was how little anywhere in Grimsby required his particular field of expertise. As months went by, he grew increasingly desperate as employment eluded him. He updated his CV almost every week and as the realisation dawned that he was too over-qualified for the positions available, he reluctantly removed his master's degree from the résumé. Several months later he also removed his bachelor's degree and A-levels too. This seemed to work as he gained employment in a local fish factory on a small amount above the minimum wage.

Terry regretted the decisions he'd made and whilst he very much still loved Shelley, he resented her for his current situation. He realised it wasn't her fault and that she wouldn't have been able to predict the outcome, but wished she'd attempted to stay in Bristol as opposed to going back to the security of the family bosom. Terry drank in the rock bars in Grimsby town centre, wanting to obliterate all the negative thoughts around his situation and fell in with Jake's crowd by default. He considered Jake to be a gobshite and when he referred to him as 'Scotch' he'd too quickly growled a correction to 'Scottish' causing uproarious laughter from Jake and his pals as it became clear that Jake deliberately made the 'mistake' as a wind up. After that point he would forever be known as 'Scotch Terry' something he grew more comfortable with as his fondness for the group continued.

The name seemed to take on a sinister double meaning as his frequent drinking sessions eventually descended into full-blown alcoholism, something he'd tried to mask from Shelley and her family. After his child, Garth, (named after the character from Wayne's World, the film he and Shelley watched repeatedly during their early months together) was born, Terry moved his family into a small terraced rented house onto Willows Housing Estate, notorious among locals for being a 'rough' area. He was saddened by what he perceived as a worsening of his situation and his drinking grew to a point he could no longer hide it anymore. Shelley, despite the love she felt for him knew Garth shouldn't be raised in that kind of environment moved back to her parents' house, whilst Terry vowed to stay in Grimsby to always be there for his newly born son.

He tried frequently to stop drinking and one of the last times he hung around with Jake and his crowd was when Jake organised a 'sobriety intervention' at Terry's home, bringing friends and large quantities of alcohol round. Terry was deeply offended by this, although he'd let none of them know he'd a severe drinking problem; that they didn't respect his decisions made him distance himself from them even more. He drank with them anyway and actually enjoyed the company and after this point decided that abstinence would never work, but regulating his intake might be more effective. Over the weeks that followed he reduced his two bottles of spirits to one, then half, to a few measured glasses per day, keeping any severe hangovers and withdrawal away. The whole time his once soft Glaswegian accent became distinctly more guttural and prominent and he realised he'd conformed to a rather negative stereotype.

It was one of these measured glasses he sipped as he settled on a BBC show about the universe with Brian Cox. He pondered if he would have ever been in a similar position to him and if it was possible to ever try for his doctorate as he still harboured a passion for the science. It was something he largely had to ignore with the people around as they'd no knowledge of the subject to discuss it at the same level, nor did they have the interest. Angered by his poor life choices and what he viewed as Brian Cox's smug face on the screen he shouted angrily

-    Away wi' ye! Ye fuckin' posey wee pretty boy so y'are!

The venting didn't help and for the first time in months Terry thought about Jake and his friends. He couldn't figure out what association his mind made to bring them to the forefront of it or why he would think about them right now. He was interrupted by his mobile ringing with an unfamiliar number.

- Aye, whae is this?
- Terry, It's Jim
- Aye, y'alreet? Whit is it yir wantin'?
- Look, it's really weird. Jake has gone missing. I'm with Pete and the last time I saw him he told me to come to you, as you know about this sort of thing.
- Whit sort ay thing?
- I really can't explain over the phone. I realise we haven't seen you for a while, but is it ok if we come over to talk?
- Ah'm no in the mood fir a perty!
- It isn't like that. Neither are we. We just need to talk. It's something you're apparently an expert in according to Jake.
- Aye. C'moan round.
- Cheers fella, much appreciated.

For the first time in a long time people referred to him as an expert in something. Terry considered tidying up, but then thought 'Fuck 'em. Why bother?' and mused over what they would be coming round to discuss. He considered the coincidence he'd thought about them only moments before, he suddenly had a notion about what they wanted to speak about. Except it couldn't be… surely that was just theoretical…?

Chapter 17.

Jake stood back at the bar in the Matrix club eyeing the pool table area intently. Sure enough, as he'd somehow already seen, his friends drifted away leaving Sarah stood by herself. He viewed Scrobbo catching onto this and to Jake's amusement, smooth down imaginary creases in his tracksuit top and make his way over. As before, his body positioning was blocking any potential 'escape routes' for Sarah and she again looked uncomfortable. If it were anyone else, he would have allowed this scene to play itself out, but Sarah meant something to him and he couldn't allow it to continue.

He strode over and positioned himself between Sarah and Scrobbo. He didn't consider the way he dealt with this situation before was a good idea. In fact, he realised he'd been quite offensive.

- Scrobbo is it?
- It's Derek. Fuck you want?
- If you have to pin a bird in the corner to speak to her, then she doesn't want that conversation. Capiche?

Sarah winced at Jake saying 'bird'. She hated that, and besides, it implied a relationship they didn't have. Derek glowered at Jake.

- You fucking what?

- Capiche means understand. You must excuse me, I'm not fluent in cretin.

Rage took over of Derek's body. He despised people talking down to him and as had been evident in his past, he'd poor impulse control and lacked to the reasoning skills to react in any other way than to lash out. He swung a nearby empty bottle of Newcastle Brown at Jake's head, disappointed by the fact it didn't break. Sarah screamed at him to fuck off, but he wouldn't be denied as he rained heavy blows upon the now prone and dazed figure of Jake. Realising his fists were not doing as much damage as he would like to Jake's back, he changed to kicks and stomps as Jake groggily tried to scramble closer to the pool table instinctively for more protection. Derek's kicks made their way through Jake's arms covering his head frequently and the sole of his trainers tore the skin above his eye, causing large amounts of blood to spurt on the floor and table. The bouncers, being alerted by the raised voices ran to intervene; the whole incident so far lasting seconds rather than minutes and dragged the upper half of his body away, whilst he continued to kick at a target no longer in his reach. As Derek was being dragged past the bar to the exit, a person beyond his vision reported the incident to the police, so he allowed his body to relax for a moment and as he was taken out of the door, the bouncers' grip loosened a little, he seized the opportunity to break free into a sprint down the long, cobbled beer garden area and into the street. What was originally a surge of anger gave way to a sinking fear he would return to prison for his actions. He rounded the corner and headed down an alleyway next to the train station which had high walls and overhanging trees. The darkness of the thoroughfare allowed him to slow down and take stock of his panic. He figured that he'd at least a few minutes before police and an ambulance arrived at the club and convinced himself he hadn't hurt the guy that badly after all. He needed to get home as fast as possible, so he broke back into a run.

Derek's attempts to calm himself down were short lived, as he heard a siren surprisingly close, which led to him running as fast as he could towards the train lines. The barriers were down and lights were approaching, but he was certain he had enough time to make it across as he vaulted over the barriers onto the tracks. He may well have been correct if it wasn't for a cable, virtually invisible in the dark which caught the tongue of his trainer, causing him to stumble to the floor, the roaring sound of the train thundering through his ears as he frantically made it to his feet as the train smashed into his side sending him many feet down the track into a pole, his collision taken squarely on the back of the neck. He felt nothing but a crunching sensation from where his shattered vertebrae ground at an incorrect angle with itself. His last thought before dying were 'I can see my own arse'.

Meanwhile, Jake's friends gathered round him at the pool table in the Matrix club, wishing audibly for the death of Derek for his actions. Unaware he had escaped the bouncers, Baz roared loudly at the door 'Scrobbo, ya dead!' causing an approving impromptu lynch mob of friends to head outside. Sarah remained with Jake and turned him over and let out a sob when she looked at his face. Underneath the crimson mask, his right eye puffed out, looking as if someone had placed a mouldy peach into his broken orbital bone. His top lip had torn, flapping with each pained breath as he tried to make a joke 'you should see the other cunt'. Sarah didn't find it funny however, due to her concern, but relieved that at least he still had his wits about him as she used her sleeve to wipe his blood from his eyes.

- Ambulance is on its way Jake. Can you sit up?
- In a minute. That didn't go exactly as planned
- Don't worry about it.

Jake struggled to lean up against the wall, sat like a broken doll as Sarah helped to guide him there. His head hung as the effort seemed to drain the consciousness from his body.

Chapter 18.

Craig unlocked the doors to the Matrix as he'd done every night for the past god-knows how many years. Tonight would be different as the club was closed to the public because he'd agreed to hold a memorial service for Jake, who had now been missing for almost a year. He missed Jake as he was one of the few customers that still came in from the old days when drinking in Grimsby was the sole focus of anyone's week. Although this was still true of the younger generation, things had changed, from his point of view, significantly for the worse. Grimsby used to have a thriving rock scene and a sense of unity that dissipated in favour of the selfie generation being obsessed with only going where everyone else would be. He remembered as an underage drinker going to the now-closed Baker Street nightclub on a Wednesday and having incredible nights with only 20-30 people in the club. Matrix was busy these days, but full of wankers who held little interest in music or the rock scene in general, so he loathed them and glad that Jake agreed.

- Bastard lazy shitting cunts!

Craig yelled at no-one as he noticed the bar fridges lacking stock and a lot of the optics needing changing. The staff closing up hadn't bothered to do these perfunctory actions and as ever; he was left to do it himself. He made his way to the cellar and noticed that the empty barrels hadn't been moved either which elicited a fresh cacophony of expletives for several minutes. As he calmed down, he thought people would find him mental if they heard his stream-of-consciousness like swearing at the walls. As he exited the cellar, he realised that someone had; Pete, accompanied by Natasha, stood at the bar looking uncomfortable, whilst Natasha struggled to contain a giggling fit.

- Errr…. sorry, we're early. Just thought we would come and see if you needed a hand with anything?
- Ahh. Sorry about that. Lazy fucking kids working here. Yeah. Appreciate it. Can you stock the fridges?
- No worries. And we appreciate you letting us have tonight.
- Forget about it. The owner knows there will be a decent crowd in, and besides, Jake must have paid at least a year's worth of my salary into the bar over the last decade. Barge too.

Pete dutifully helped stock the fridges. At first he deliberately laid the bottles on their side, catching them as they rolled out, grinning at Craig for approval, who looked confused. Pete, chastised, stopped doing this and put them in properly. Pete was unfazed, he knew making veiled Reeves and Mortimer references wasn't something everyone got, but for some reason assumed that Craig would. Pete still kept an aspect of teenage 'idol worship' towards Craig, since he was one of Jake's friends from 'back in the day'. Craig actually the got the reference a moment later and smiled back at Pete, who then focussed on the task at hand.

Natasha sat yards away, contacting everyone to ensure they would arrive before a certain time as the gate doors would be locked to prevent any unwanted arguments with potential customers. She wasn't looking forward to the evening as large social gatherings intimidated her and she usually ended up sitting quietly in a corner chatting to like-minded people, waiting for the evening to end. Her original idea for putting on the evening was to help Pete get over the disappearance of his brother, yet for some reason, Pete seemed positively buoyant. She'd expected tears and a lot of moping, but not this. Whilst shocked at Pete's lightened mood, it didn't distress her, far from it. It elated her to see the jokey boy she fell in love with again. She resolved not to point out she'd noticed for fear of jinxing the situation and leading him back to his recent sullen ways.

Craig and Pete, having finished preparing the bar for the evening together, both stood at the bar with freshly poured pints. Craig, despite his earlier outburst, cherished that he managed a place like this, rather than a shitty chain-pub, where he could make autonomous decisions without having to consult an area manager, who would then have to contact a head office, who would then say no to any decision they didn't deem to be profit oriented. That tonight, he would be able to get pissed whilst working would be a bonus. He'd one other member of staff coming in, Chloe, who he would allow to do most of the work tonight as he caught up with old friends and shared stories about Jake. It was also fitting he brought Chloe in as Jake once confided in him that he had quite a thing for her, yet would never pursue it because of the fifteen year age difference between them would make him feel 'like a peado'. He hadn't agreed with this since Chloe was twenty-three (then twenty-two) and he'd often harboured similar desires himself. Jake continued that she intimidated him and often made him lost for words around her, something which never ordinarily happened to him. Craig dismissed this as faux-romantic drunken bullshit, but wondered now if he'd been genuine. As if on cue, Chloe walked through the door and headed straight behind the bar smiling at everyone. Craig thought it easy to perceive why Jake was as enamoured; she looked beautiful and both he and Pete tried not to look for too long as to appear lecherous. She headed to the corner of the bar, seeing everything done, she whipped out her mobile phone and stared at it intently. Craig then realised why he wasn't as taken with her as Jake.

Craig poured two more pints for him and Pete, paid for this time, and Natasha approached requesting one for herself. They chatted for a while whilst people filtered in and the formerly quiet room was filled with life and laughter again, except on this occasion from customers who didn't irritate him.

Chapter 19.

-    Where to mate?

Jake was disorientated. His last conscious memory was trying to act brave after the brutal beating doled out upon him by Scrobbo. His hands rose to his face and checked for damage. There remained none. He clicked his camera into 'selfie' mode to check; there wasn't a mark on him. He also noticed the day. Still Friday. Nausea swept over him as he realised that he hadn't dreamt or imagined this the first time. It was somehow real, and he wondered how to pull himself out of this.

-    C'mon mate, where you going?

The impatience of the taxi driver jolted Jake into mumbling to head to the Matrix. Jake pondered his options and decided the best way to fight the situation would be to ride it out. He knew how events would go and not to confront Scrobbo so directly when that occurred. Or perhaps he could prevent the situation from ever happening? He resolved to stay close to Sarah all night, in an attempt to ensure Scrobbo never approaches her in the first place. Or failing that, it would be possible to just ignore it. Sarah was an adult, and no doubt had far more experience rebuffing would-be suitors than he had with women. He resolved to make a judgement call should the need arise.

After arriving at Matrix, he walked past Sophie, but didn't acknowledge her. At this point, he was still a stranger to her and lacked the drunken confidence it took to spark the situation as it went the first time. To try getting through the whole time loop ordeal, he resolved to get drunker than he ever had and hoped that would take the edge off the anxiety.

He ordered a pint of vodka red-bull and six shots of Sambuca, which he then downed in rapid succession prompting Craig to arch his eyebrows and compelled him to speak.

- Take it easy there dude. I know you like a drink, but that's asking for trouble.
- Don't worry about it. Your legal obligation to warn me off is done now. I hereby remove you of any responsibility to what happens to me because of the booze you sell.
- It isn't like that mate. Just a bit of concern. Besides, if it were anything to do with obligation, I'd cut you off and refuse to serve you.
- You wouldn't fucking DARE!
- Ha haha. I don't see the point, anyway. You would only go to another pub and get served, anyway. At least I can keep my eye on you and aware on what to tell the amblyance.
- Ha! I'm the one getting trashed and you still can't say ambulance!

Craig felt a little hurt. He and Jake held a conversation a few weeks prior about it annoyed him when people mispronounced certain words. This then turned into an almost hour long conversation in which every sentence contained at least one 'thick' version of a word. Jake not getting the reference led Craig to wonder if there was more on his mind than he let on. He continued to press.

- Are you ok? This isn't like you. I mean you usually save at least one shot for wandering about.
- I suppose you could say I'm having a bad day. Or night.

Craig wanted to probe further, but the arrival of Jim and Sarah created a raucous greeting from Jake, meaning that the conversation to now be done and likely forgotten about. The worst part about running a pub was that many friendships became small pockets of exchanges like these. Working the hours that people socialised resulted in a sometimes lonely existence surrounded by people. The best times happened when the occasionally had a lock-in and he was able to enjoy their company more, but often people had left in favour of going to Gulliver's, something he never bothered doing anymore, since by the time he had closed up, there was only about half an hour left. He inwardly shrugged and considered he would likely see Jake again the following weekend, anyway.

- Hey-Ohhhhhh!!!!
- Jesus Jake, you're nearly wankered already!

- Then join me Professor Special Brew! Sarah, darling, how positively enchanting to see you! Have you put on weight? It looks good on you, unlike your hair, which is a mess. Mwah. Mwah.

Sarah was offended, not knowing if Jake was joking about the weight gain and messy hair or not. She decided to treat it as a joke and responded in kind.

- Mwah. Mwah. Charmed, I'm sure. You stink quite badly this evening and I don't reckon any woman in her right mind would ever contemplate sleeping with you!

Jake stared coldly at her for a moment.

- The fuck is that supposed to mean?

'Shit', panicked Sarah. 'I thought he was joking'. Sarah then started putting two and two together and realised that if he wasn't joking, he intended to be mean about weight gain and crap hair. She stammered out an apologetic, yet angry reply when he burst out laughing. He had fooled her again. The twat.

- Your face! Ahahaha!
- Piss off! Cunt! Hahaha

Sarah was relieved, but still considered that it crossed a line, uncharacteristically for her. But still she was swept up in the 'Jake show' and started quickly consuming drinks in a futile attempt to catch up. She became distracted by a woman in a dressing gown barged past her, close to tears. Jake looked sad and shouted after her.

-    Sophie, get changed! It will all be all right!

She didn't acknowledge his response but noticed Jake deep in thought. She was unaware what was currently happening to him and her initial observation about him shouting after the dressing gown clad woman to be him taking the piss. Jake meanwhile realised he had the ability to have prevented this by being an arsehole for two minutes and whilst he wasn't particularly bonded with Sophie, he would much rather make someone angry than make them sad. Anger easily subsided, yet sadness lingered. He wasn't the cause, but was able to be the solution, which stood the same in his eyes. He contemplated the Scrobbo/ Sarah scenario, and that prompted him to stick with her for the rest of the evening.

The rest of the night continued, over to the pool table as it had before. Jake had ensured he had enough drinks to prevent wandering off to the bar and idly chatted with Sarah as the rest of their friends filtered away as they had done twice before in Jake's world. He eyed Scrobbo over at the bar area and noticed him looking at Sarah as if waiting for him to leave. Rashly, he grabbed her by the waist and kissed her. This didn't have quite the effect he had hoped.

-    What the fuck are you doing?

Sarah angrily pushed him away and became furious. She hated anyone taking liberties like this, the kiss being an assault to her; the sexual equivalent of a sucker-punch.

- What makes you think you can do that? We've been friends for years and then you do that shit?
- I er... er... had my reasons. I didn't mean to piss you off.

Jake wanted to explain, but just couldn't. He'd barely begun to understand the situation he was in and knew, despite his drunken poor judgement, telling her what was going on wouldn't result in her believing him or accepting it as a reason. He tried meekly explaining how he saw Scrobbo's predatory eye on her from the bar.

- That guy, Scrobbo, he was looking over at you. He's dodgy...
- What? You reckon I can't handle some guy looking at me? I've been telling losers to fuck off ever since I got tits. I don't need you shoving your fucking tongue in my mouth against my will to aid me in that department!

Sarah noted that Jake looked thoroughly dejected and embarrassed. Despite her anger, she also felt remorse at getting so angry at him, but she had boundaries that needed firmly keeping in place. She softened her tone and the volume of her voice.

\- You're hammered. I get that. I'm disappointed in you Jake. I trust that you are one of the few guys I know to not blindside me with teenage shit like that. I'll chalk it up to how fucking drunk you are this time, but be warned; you EVER try shit like that with me again, I will never speak to you again. Ever. Got it?

Jake nodded, chastised. He looked at the bar and acknowledged that Scrobbo's focus was on another potential victim. At least it worked. No consolation for him though as this potentially could destroy their friendship. They remained stood together although silently sipping their drinks. Sarah hated this and contemplated going home as there was no way the evening would stop being awkward for her now.

Jake sneered, 'fuck it'. I'll do it differently next time.

Chapter 20.

The memorial of sorts for Jake in the Matrix club was in full swing. The jukebox in heavy use and the club was full. Craig left the bar tending duties to Chloe and mingled with old friends and acquaintances. Despite the sadness of the occasion for many, people seemed determined to have a good time, often sounding the clichéd 'It's what he would have wanted' as a reason.

Jim, Sarah, Natasha and Pete settled into a corner, sat sharing stories about Jake from his distant past and Craig opted to join them. As he listened, he realised that he never really knew him that well and only saw one side to his personality. He'd seen a change over the years, what was once just an outgoing person laughing his way through an evening, he saw a snide bully often emerge, someone who derived laughter at the expense of others. Craig often put this down to drunkenness and noticed people behave in a far worse manner over the years. At least he used words and not his fists. Clumsily, he tried to ask why this change came about.

- What happened to him? He got a lot nastier as years carried on.

Pete looked incensed, whilst Jim raised a quizzical eyebrow.

- Y'know what I mean. I loved the guy to bits and everything, but could never shake the notion that something bothered him all the time after a point.

Jim looked around the table and sensed that it ok to talk about the things that Jake kept to himself. Jim had often been his confidante, listening to things Jake never wanted to burden his brother with. Jim was aware that Sarah had no clue about his past and her ears pricked up at the prospect of finding out. Jake had always been good at rapidly changing the topic of discussion if he felt uncomfortable, often distracting people with a barbed put-down directed at others; the resulting laughter being ample to de-rail any conversation. Jake remained the undisputed king of communication hand grenades.

- Yeah, I know what you mean Craig. It's a long story. Fuck it, I'll tell you, I'm sure wherever he is he wouldn't mind at this point. Y'know he owned that record shop years back yeah?
- Yeah, I spent a fair few quid there myself.
- Sarah, you might not have known. Back in the nineties he used to spend hundreds in a local record shop. He could browse vinyl for hours and he got to knowing a fair bit about values and stuff. The guy that ran the place decided he wanted out and basically offered to sell his entire stock for a couple of grand. Jake snapped him up and maxed out his credit card and overdraft to buy it all and carried

on running the shop as he was unemployed. Fun fact—he never did pay off those debts, he just moved. Anyway, he did ok for a while. A huge building, three storeys included in the lease and it was only the shop that got used. They stated in the lease he couldn't live there and he wanted to use the extra space for something. Oh yeah, he lost custom because of the internet and stuff, fewer people buying and selling music physically, so he needed money. He threw a party in the upstairs, charging a few quid for people to get in, he had the music and everything and someone had sold him some DJ equipment on the cheap before, so he used the first floor to host this event and he made hundreds. People he'd never met turned up because everyone was going, and since people brought their own booze, it didn't count as a club or something. It was probably well illegal. Anyway, he saw this and did it again, weekly after a time, he bought soundproofing stuff and ended up using both floors as it got so busy. He loved every minute and ended up barely opening his shop after that, two days a week and then throw the party nights. Then he spent the rest of the week getting wasted and just doing whatever he liked.

Sarah was astounded. She was aware he'd previously owned a record shop, but he'd never mentioned it. Craig already knew all of this however, he'd gone to the parties when he wasn't working. He'd also been told the parties annoyed the pub landlords as they affected the custom levels. He wondered why Jake stopped.

- So why did he stop?
- That's the thing. He never wanted to. Jake said it wouldn't last forever. He started getting a load of grief from the council and despite his best efforts, there was no way to hide it. They put pressure on the leaseholder who eventually ended up not allowing him to renew his lease. He went from having everything to having nothing and he had been frivolous with the cash, so kept no savings. Never one to look to the future. He tried to take the nights to other places, but never had the same vibe in pubs as they were too regulated. Then the gold-digging bitch he was with at the time dumped him, basically because he didn't have the money to keep her anymore, or indeed, the status that made it important to be 'seen' with him in the 'scene'. He was broken up about all of that.

Sarah had tried several times to talk about his previous relationships. She grew intrigued by the possibility of finally being able to garner information on this.

- Wasn't he married?
- Yeah, that ended, they got married young: it didn't work. He was devastated at the time, but realised 'it is what it

is'. That never got to him long-term, the failed marriage was the impetus behind him rushing into a relationship with that gold-digger though. He desperately wanted to jump into the same level of relationship he had with his ex-wife, without having the slow burn that leads up to it and she took full advantage of that fact...

Jim got interrupted by Craig pointing to the security camera footage. Hammering on the back gates and occasionally glowering at the camera stood Scrobbo.

Chapter 21.

Jake leaned against the railings outside the Barge in his favourite brooding spot. His clumsy attempt to kiss Sarah bothered him and he'd stopped drinking for the evening. A combination of the knowledge he'd upset and disappointed her with the rejection had sobered him up immensely. He was aware that the evening would repeat itself and no-one would be any the wiser about his actions, but he didn't want to face Sarah again because of the shame. He started the cold walk home, neglecting to go inside to inform his friends of his departure. As he reached the perimeter of the Barge's beer garden, Sarah emerged from the pub and shouted after him.

- Jake! Where are you going?
- Home. Look, I'm so sorry ok. It's a weird night. I shouldn't have done that. It's awful I've pissed you off and...
- Don't be stupid! I was angry at the time, but I'm not even giving it a second thought now.

Sarah paused. Curious more than angry at this point and wondered where the clumsy attempt came from. She pressed the situation.

- Why though? We've been friends for years and you've done nothing like that. Why now?
- It's hard to explain.

- Try.
- Really hard to explain.
- Really try.
- You won't believe me.
- Now you're making matters worse.
- Ok. In a nutshell. This evening has happened twice now. Scrobbo started basically menacing you, so I pretended to be retarded and we ended up fucking. Second time I got in his face and got a kicking and you got upset. Basically, I got the impression it was you who had feelings for me.

Sarah stood silently. Anger swelled in her chest as she couldn't believe that he tried to piss about and wind her up at a time when she wanted a serious answer. It suddenly dawned on her that all the jokes he made weren't shared, he usually laughed at her expense and held no respect for her whatsoever. Jake, unaware of this, continued.

- I don't know if there is a tomorrow, there's a chance I'm hallucinating or having some vivid dream or whatever...
- Fuck off.
- What?
- Go home. You fucking prick. I asked you a serious question and you take the piss like this. I can't believe it has taken me so long to realise what an arsehole you are, how little you give a shit about me.

- Eh? What the fuck Sarah! I'm telling you the absolute truth! I'm not trying to wind you up, I wouldn't...
- Piss off! You ALWAYS wind me up, then have a giggle later, but this is different! You crossed a line and now made a joke out of it. Well no more. Get fucked off home. I don't want to speak to you anymore
- Sarah! Please...

Sarah abruptly turned and re-entered the pub, holding up her middle finger as she departed, leaving Jake teary eyed and dejected. He wanted to follow her and try to convince her he told the truth, but her rancour intimidated him. He'd never seen her that mad at anyone, least of all him. Jake fought back a sob he turned and walked. Two minutes later, it rained furiously, the icy February winds making each drop painfully stinging to his face. He pulled his hoodie as tight to his face as possible and tried to consider ways of rectifying the situation. Like the rain as he walked home, he mused it would be 'typical' if this happened at the end of his repeating evening; left with a huge mess with no way out.

He considered what would happen if this evening continued repeatedly. Was he around tomorrow? He imagined not, but wasn't certain. His internal logic told him that if this was some sort of loop, he was trapped in it, existing only in this evening. Childishly, he sneered, 'that will make her feel bad about this'. Jake then considered he didn't want Sarah to suffer in any way, she'd done nothing wrong.

As he entered his flat, he became glad of the shelter from the freezing rain. He took off his soaking clothes and went to the bathroom to dry his hair, unsuccessfully trying to avoid the gaze of the bathroom mirror that reflected a bloated pink mess that revolted him. 'No fucking wonder she was pissed off' he stared bitterly at his reflection. One reason he liked to drink so much was that it let him forget for a few precious hours what he looked like and it gave him confidence to act like a much more attractive person.

He made his way to bed and wished hard that he was still trapped in a time-loop; that this evening didn't happen and he'd a chance to do it over. He realised that telling people what was happening couldn't be an option, as Sarah proved, they would accuse him of making it up to amuse himself, until tomorrow of course, but by then it would be too late.

It occurred to him it would now be impossible to visit his family. His parents were on holiday, due to get back late Saturday. He wondered if there was a fixed time when things 'reset' or if the night ended when he slept. Being that the evening started again after he lost consciousness from the Scrobbo kicking, he hypothesised it to be the latter. He vowed to stay awake as he possessed an urge to see his family stronger than he'd ever had. Sunday was when he'd planned to visit, but the likelihood of him staying awake another 48 hours was slim. He also had a craving to see his brother Pete, so if the evening reset, he would bail on the night out and visit him and Natasha instead.

His plan to stay awake in place, he spent several hours binge watching TV shows on Netflix. This proved difficult as his mind raced about his circumstances, but after a short while he got invested in the antics of the Entourage crew. He struggled to keep his eyes open and awoke with a start after falling asleep for a second.

- Where to mate?

Back again in the taxi, clothed and sober Jake cursed.

- Fuck!

Chapter 22.

Craig re-entered The Matrix Club after disposing of Scrobbo. He did this quickly and efficiently, eager to get back to Jim telling his stories, or gossip, about Jake's past. Jim had always been a natural story-teller and had a way about his delivery that kept it interesting and humorous. Jim paused the story, intrigued by the possibility of drama concerning the scratter, Scrobbo.

- What did that cunt want?
- Just trying to get in. He'd heard what's going on and tried to claim he's mates with Jake.
- Haha. Doubt it. Jake hates chavvy scum.
- True. Anyway. You said about Jake's ex and stuff?

Jim beamed with pride. He loved being the focus of other people's attention, no matter the circumstances. Not out of ego, but a desire to entertain, a trait he considered he shared with Jake. Aware that even Pete was not privy to some information, he tried to skirt any retro-active offence Jake's brother may have felt.

- So, before I carry on, Pete, some of this even you don't know. Jake never told you as you had your own stuff to go through at the time and he didn't want to burden you with his problems. Afterwards, he never wanted to talk about it; he buried it and left it in the past. Or he tried to. I reckon it affected all of his decisions all the time and made him way more guarded than he ever used to be. Jake had a lot of anger there he never vented.

Pete grew a little upset Jake hadn't told him everything. He'd known bad stuff happened to Jake in relation to his ex-girlfriends, but whenever he asked about it he'd always replied 'she's a cunt' and left it there. It made sense as Pete was broken up about his first girlfriend during that time and had troubles with work and Natasha the second time Jake's relationship ended. He smiled and dismissively waved to allow Jim to continue, which he was more than happy to do.

- Yeah, so anyway, Jake succeeded, albeit not in a traditional tax-paying sense. Pete, y'know his folks constantly got at him to get a 'proper' job, but he stayed determined to make things work on his terms. He broke up with his wife before everything really took off, but he missed her a lot, he wanted the same level of intimacy again as I'd said. Enter Clarice. I mean most of you remember how fucking stunning she looked?

Everyone except Sarah nodded. She'd only known Jake during the last few years and he'd been single the whole time. He'd offered no information about his previous partners and she hadn't been motivated to ask. She looked quizzically at Jim, who picked up on her visual cue and described her.

- Make no bones about it, she was model material. Long blonde straight hair down her back, full lips and a cracking set of tits. She approached him whilst he was doing one of his nights. He wasn't stupid, he was aware she's way out of his league looks-wise. He jumped at the opportunity to get with her, because like most guys there, he fancied her. Thing is, it's true what they say about beauty only being skin deep. He still pined for his ex-wife, but wanted to move on and be as close to someone else. So they got a place together after only a month, it seemed pretty ok for a while. After they did their 'settling in', he had folks round again and we saw what a nasty person she is. Jake would be the first to admit he wasn't perfect, and he made loads of gaffes along the way. He kept calling her his ex-wife's name for a while. Not intentionally, it slipped out once when he got drunk and she hit the fucking roof, way more than necessary. He stayed up all night arguing about that one. Because of that, it kind of imprinted on his brain so he kept accidentally doing it. To my knowledge, he didn't do it during sex though.

Sarah winced at the idea of a guy doing the same thing to her. She tried to imagine how she would feel and how she would react. She liked to think she wouldn't be overly sensitive about it, certainly not to the point of long drawn out arguments. Jim continued his diatribe.

- That was only the start. I was round there every night for a while. He used to have lots of visitors back then, mostly younger people wanting association with someone who in their minds was a 'big deal'. I guess Clarice was one of them too, she was eighteen when he got with her and Jake would often put her histrionics down to her being younger than him, being twenty five. Anyway, she basically told him every day he was ugly; that she was playing 'pull a pig' with her mates and won. I mean we all tried to take it as a joke, but it's a joke that wore thin pretty damned quick. She would constantly accuse him of cheating on her, totally baseless shit. She spent literally most of her time with him. They lived together, she always was with him when he went out, yet berated him for imagined trysts not possible unless he could be in two places at once. And those arguments would fucking RAGE man. People were jealous as fuck of him being with her and loads of people would be like 'you can do better' or worse, make stuff up to try to split them up. She would go to a shop and come back screaming at him about something someone 'told' her. It would start with him trying to calmly get her to focus on facts like 'when' it happened and apart from her visits to family or shopping, on his fucking dime I might add, he couldn't have been able to fuck anyone else, not without her seeing it with her own eyes. Then he would inevitably get mad after a few hours of her deliberately ignoring basic frigging logic and then she would change tact and harangue him about calling her his ex-wife's name which would put him 'on the ropes'. Safe to say, this wasn't the idyllic romance he wanted.

Craig nodded in acknowledgment. He'd seen some of their rows erupt when they'd been out in the past. He hadn't envied the embarrassing shouted outbursts she favoured and saw Jake leaving, not wanting to have his personal business humiliate him in public. Pete hadn't really remembered those times since. He always assumed at the time relationships were like that, being a teenager himself at the time. Looking back, he saw it to be pretty rough and regretted the friendship he'd shown to Clarice. Despite them being a similar age, he often referred to her as his big sister. He knew, on balance, there had to be good times too, but it definitely wasn't a healthy set of circumstances to be in.

- Anyway, the part most don't know is around this time, he'd decided he wasn't happy. She kissed an acquaintance of his at one of his nights and he ended it there and then. But then a woman came into his life who was nice to him, pretty and she seemed to genuinely like him. He'd told her he was in a relationship, to make it clear to her, but he liked her too. She turned up to every party he put on. After he finished it with Clarice, he took the plunge and met her for a date. They'd been chatting a fair bit the weeks prior. Cut a long story short, they slept together, and it looked like something further would happen. Then Clarice got in touch wanting to 'talk'. She goes round a few days after they split up and insisted the guy forced himself on her, but the worst part; she told Jake she loved him, which she hadn't done before and this changed everything for him. He suddenly reckoned she was what he wanted and abruptly ended things with the other woman, I forget her name. Now Clarice was pretty, but also extremely clever too. Manipulatively clever. And egotistical to boot. My theory is she couldn't stand the fact that it ended with her being the 'villain' and she knew how painful Jake's marriage breakup was, so she manipulated him into getting back together based on the fact he wanted someone to actually love him again.

Jim paused as if to let the dramatic point sink in. Content it had, he continued.

- Problem was, like an idiot, Jake never mentioned the fact this rendezvous with the other lass happened. And in this quaint little fishing hamlet known as GY, these things can never stay a secret, especially when every cunt wants to bang your missus.

Chapter 23.

Jake had grown despondent as he sat in the hull area of the Barge Inn. It was unusual for him to ever settle in any pub on a night out, preferring to be on his feet and on the move. He considered himself beaten. This was, by his count, the fortieth time he'd experienced this same evening. He'd tried to stay awake to be able to visit his brother and parents, but even a slight micro sleep resulted in the 'taxi awakening'. Time for him, stood at a standstill and there was little new in the form of entertainment that interested him, he'd yet to make it beyond midday on the Saturday. He missed his family terribly and tried to console himself with the fact that at least he got to spend a lot of time with his friends. The problem being that the conversations were ultimately the same and began to bore him.

After Sarah's angry outburst, despite the knowledge she would have no memory of it, Jake appeared awkward around her and desperately wanted the affection she showed towards him on the first time the night played itself out. He mistakenly assumed she'd found him more attractive because he'd pretended to be handicapped to get rid of the menace Scrobbo; being a creative, but horrendous way of dealing with a situation that could easily result in conflict. But despite doing this repeatedly several times, the same situation never arose.

Jake eventually figured that it wasn't just that incident that caused her to change her feelings towards him. He'd forgotten about the Sophie incident and began re-creating that scenario too. The combination of fearlessness and the possibility of him potentially having another person interested worked. He moderated his drink and picked up on the cues he'd missed the first time around and ended up back at Sarah's flat, content he'd made more effort with his sexual performance each subsequent time, noting each time what she liked and disliked.

Then it seemed different. Jake developed stronger feelings towards Sarah, seeing her as almost a soulmate. To her, each night was the first time, but to him it became a relationship and as such, their feelings towards each other fell out of sync. She'd been put off by his nature, finding him clingy after they'd fucked. Jake noticed this and although it pained him to do it, he had to stop as the closeness he displayed got rebuffed and treated as if it were intrusive. For the first time in years, Jake had a connection to someone on a deeper level, yet knew it had no future, as he had no future. He had only the present with a bitch of a past.

The last time he slept with her, he kissed her goodbye as he left, struggling to fight back tears knowing it to be the last time. He saw how weird she considered him to be and was sure he'd made the right decision. This was three 'nights' ago, but to her, none of it ever happened. He felt lost and didn't know how long he could carry on living this one night over and over again, or if there was any way out. Jake briefly considered suicide, but didn't want to hurt the people he loved more than he did yesterday, forty nights ago.

Jake stood at the bar and bought a few bottles of 'alco-piss', the blue vodka based drink he remained such a fan of, yet was the subject of massive derision from his peers. He'd decided to go somewhere quiet to contemplate without distraction and stashed the bottles in the deep pockets of his coat. As he walked, he cursed himself for forgetting about the rain and waddled to the shelter of the town hall archway. The steps remained dry and offered a place to sit, the dirty-beige concrete looking cleaner than it should, being the entrance to a civic building. He placed the bottles next to him and contemplated his next move, or if he actually had a next move at all.

Lost in thought he failed to spot the figure of Scrobbo emerge next to him, his tracksuit drenched and hugging his skin like wet toilet paper.

- I know you're not retarded.

Startled Jake turned and saw Scrobbo. Jake, being overweight and prone, was aware there'd be no escape and prepared himself for the kicking that would no doubt result in a taxi-wake-up. He also didn't care, knowing any pain he felt would be brief. Although to his astonishment, Scrobbo simply sat down next to him.

- I fucking hate the rain. Not exactly the clothes for it.
- Scrobbo? What the fuck do you want this time?
- My name's Derek!
- Derek then. What the fuck do you want?

Jake saw something he'd never noticed before. Derek's face was contorted, not with aggression, but with a look that almost seemed hurt.

- I hate being called Scrobbo.
- To be frank, your likes and dislikes are not high on my list of fucking concerns! I'll ask again; what in the fuck do you want?

Jake almost goaded Derek into attacking. He didn't have the energy to attempt to talk himself out of a confrontation, nor did he have much care for self-preservation. He wanted to meet this head on. Again, it surprised him that his manner wasn't responded to in kind. Derek briefly tensed, but sighed.

- Nothing. It's raining, it's dry here.
- It's dry in a lot of places. Try those.
- Yeah, why aren't you in them then?

Jake couldn't reply. He didn't want to chat with anyone, least of all this person who he despised. He declined to answer and took a swig from his bottle. Derek also sat in silence staring intently at the raindrops making the pavement out of their unwillingly shared space seem alive. With every passing moment of quiet, Jake grew angrier at the intrusion, but also curious. He'd made it clear he hated this guy, yet he still wanted to sit here with him. Was he planning an attack or mugging, psyching himself up for it and making sure there are no witnesses? Why else would you sit with a person who loathes you? He lit a cigarette, expecting the inevitable cadging to come, to which he would respond with a curt 'fuck off'. Derek saw this and pulled out a damp packet of his own. His lighter sodden too; Derek persistently tried sparking a flame. Jake sat amused by this briefly, overtaken by pity, as Derek continued to do so for well over a minute. Jake then sparked a flame of his own and proffered it towards the cigarette dangling limply from Derek's mouth.

- Cheers.
- Don't thank me. The noise irritated me.

They resumed their antagonistic silence. Both staring ahead at nothing in particular. Jake sat uncomfortable and would much rather trade insults and accept whatever came from this, but Derek wouldn't bite. He also didn't want his put-downs to be seen as 'matey banter'. He decided the best course of action would be to brave the icy rain and simply go somewhere else and prepared to stand when Derek broke the verbal fast.

- Why do you take the piss out of me?

'Oh Jesus', thought Jake, 'here we fucking go'.

Chapter 24.

In the Matrix Club, Jim held court to a captive audience still with his tales of Jake's previous relationship experiences. Part of him wished he'd told more people this before, especially the times when Jake pissed people off, if only to try to explain where his anger and bitterness came from when he got inebriated. After a brief pause to buy drinks from the increasingly swamped Chloe, he continued.

- So, yeah. Jake shagged some lass and got manipulated back into a relationship with Clarice. And he didn't tell her it happened, which in all fairness, was a pretty shitty thing to do, but he reckoned he got back the relationship he wanted again, he was scared to put it all in jeopardy over something that happened whilst they weren't together. He completely cut communication with the other woman, told her what happened and left it at that, there was no subterfuge or sneaking around, his tryst with the woman ended.

Sarah considered how she would have been in the same situation. She'd always been pretty relaxed about her own exes and their past. Lying, or omitting things seemed a pretty big deal though whatever the reason to her, yet she also assumed she would never have been so mean as to constantly berate a person she was involved with romantically. 'So yeah, fuck her. Bitch' she spat to herself. Jim carried on with his long tale.

- A couple of months went past and someone told her he'd banged this other chick. Just so happened to be the guy Clarice got off with which led to them splitting in the first place. Co-incidence, eh? But, yeah, Jake stupidly denied it and she wouldn't let it go and move on or anything. A few other people started coming out of the woodwork and kept 'confirming' it. Interestingly, since Jake hadn't been bragging or anything and the woman in question didn't move in the same circles, there was no way all these people telling tales actually knew anything about it. They simply nodded and confirmed her rants when Jake stood out of earshot. Some of these cunts were supposed to be his friends too, or at least pretended to be until they reckoned they might get a shag off his missus. I really started to hate her around then. Whenever Jake wasn't around she would slag him off in a really nasty way, such a two-faced cow, but people are shit and will basically lie to get what they want, even though the thing they lied about turned out to be true.

Pete, Sarah and Craig all looked puzzled at his last point and Jim clarified Clarice asked everyone she could if Jake cheated on her, to which a few confirmed, despite not knowing it to be true. Satisfied everyone understood his point, he prepared to continue with a slight fear his drunkenness would affect his ability to tell his stories as the evening continued. He attempted to take a re-assuring swig of Desperado, but forgetting he hadn't removed the lime, he dribbled beer all down his chin and top. A wave of laughter erupted from the table and he felt mild embarrassment, but simply grinned and carried on, ignoring his clumsiness.

- So Jake eventually came clean about it. Told Clarice what had gone on before, how he wasn't happy and was plain angry with her for getting off with the other guy. In his mind they were done, and he'd moved on, albeit quickly. He tried to placate her and say when she said she loved him; it changed everything, because before that point, it seemed like she didn't give a fuck about him and continued stringing him along. For once, she seemed pretty reasonable about it, she said she was angry he'd lied and he hadn't given her a choice about getting back together. When he told me she said that, I kind of hit the roof, because she'd gone to him begging to get back together, not the other way around, but as I said, I hated her. Jake knew I hated her and kind of ignored any advice I gave him when it came to his relationship, so there was nothing I could do. But he basically let it slide and apologised and professed to love her too. He wasn't aware at that point about all the nasty shit she said about him behind his back, but their home-life had quietened down. Since getting back together she'd almost stopped calling him ugly and shit every day, probably because she had the knowledge he was prepared to end it and she couldn't get away with it. Boy, that quickly fucking changed after this point.

Pete realised Clarice probably kept the worst things she said about Jake out of earshot of him, knowing he would tell him. As much as he'd liked Clarice at the time, family trumped all of that and in his youth he'd idolised his older brother. In some ways it never really ended, but was tempered with a sense of realism. He knew Jake possessed flaws, everyone did, but he considered Jake's positives far outweighed the negatives. Jim's brow furrowed as he resumed speaking.

-   Now he'd 'confessed his sins', Clarice basically owned the upper hand. She knew she was back in control of the relationship and all the nastiness at home started again. She bickered with him about everything and the second she was on the losing end of any argument–BOOM! She would crack out the other woman shit and attack him with it. And not verbally anymore, she started hitting him often too. Jake can take a punch and she wasn't a big woman, but no-one likes getting hit. I saw this myself a couple of times, she would start straight up punching him and he would grab her arms or something to stop her, so she would scream bloody murder about how he was 'abusing' her and implied him to be some kind of woman beater for restraining her. He told me this happened twice a week at least and he was mortified, because she drew so much attention to herself, seemingly wanting everyone to hear their business, or at least the part where she painted him as the bastard and her blameless. I kept telling him, 'get rid of the twat, she is no good and causes you nothing but pain'. But he put it down to me despising her like I said and still ignored me. Thankfully, she fucked off to university after a while to Leeds and everything calmed down a lot. They carried on being together for a couple of years, him paying for her to come back and stuff, but during the entire time, she refused to have sex with him or even have any level of intimacy and also refused to ever discuss why, which he never pressed because he didn't want the humiliating arguments, he carried on, glad of the peace. Of course she would randomly accuse him of cheating on her, tried setting him up a couple of times too, the mental cow. Got other women to come on to him to see what he would do and to his credit, he never fell for it. When she told him about it, she would say it proved nothing as he'd 'figured out' what she was doing. But she encouraged the expensive gifts and meals out, day trips and cash bungs he gave her. The only reason she stayed with him I reckon. When his business started to slow, and he became skint, she was all like 'this isn't working anymore' and ended it.

- I wish he would have told me all this at the time. I'm his brother and I'm pissed off now I gave that cow the time of day!

- Don't be pissed off mate, y'know Jake was never one to burden everyone else with his troubles, especially you. He never wanted you to be worrying about him. Jake kind of saw it as his 'job' to worry about you. Older brother syndrome and all that.

- So why did he tell you?

- Never one-sided; I told him all my shit too. Everything. I'd ring him at three or four in the morning fucked up about some shit or other and he would always answer and listen. The same in reverse for him as well. Two fuck-ups basically swapping horror stories over time. Thing is, he was always great at giving advice, but never good at taking it. Too headstrong, he always reckoned he could 'fix' things rather than accept them to be broken. A theme continuing when he got with the next one.

A wave of emotion washed over Pete. Partially due to the revelations about what Jake had gone through, but most importantly the frequent use of past tense in the conversations about his brother. He staggered towards the toilet, trying not to run before the tears came. He cursed inwardly as he saw other people in the toilets. After a curt nod of acknowledgement, he entered the cubicle as the sobs began. To disguise the sounds, he blew his nose until satisfied the toilet was empty; the silent heaves racking his body erupted into an audible cry.

Chapter 25.

- I mean, calling me Scrobbo. Why?

Jake sighed. If this was leading up to something, he wished Scrobbo/ Derek would get on with it. His contempt for Derek grew with the implication that somehow this sinewy thug could portray himself as some kind of victim. He wearily answered, hoping his response would jar the inevitable kicking he expected would come.

- It's your name isn't it?
- No, it's not my name! It's something people called me all my fucking life to take the piss out of me!

Jake realised this actually made sense and let out an involuntary laugh. In Grimsby, 'Scrob' did indeed refer to a scruff bag, a loser or a ne'er-do-well. Derek appeared to fulfil all of those categories.

- Ah. Makes sense why you get all pissy about it then. I wasn't at school with you, was I? I guess someone along the way 'introduced' you as that. I reckoned you owned an unfortunate surname.
- Well, I don't. I grew up on the Nunny, Mam on benefits, Dad in and out of nick until he fucked off for good with some bag-head. She never could afford decent clothes for

me, so even at a povvo school on the Nunny, I was the skeffy one.

Derek's tone didn't appear to contain any threat to it. Jake remained silent and considered it must have been rough, Nunny being the local nickname for the Nunsthorpe, a former council estate now owned largely by some housing association, meaning little about the residents changed, but their rents increased. It had always possessed a notoriety about it for being a rough area, although as the years passed by, much of the residential parts of Grimsby had gone a similar way. It was now easier to point out the decent areas, of which few remained. Derek continued uninterrupted.

- I mean look at you, you got it easy. You've got money, you can afford decent gear and everything. I can't get a job, no-one wants someone out of the jail. I can't even hang around with my old mates as part of my conditions...
- The fuck do you mean 'I got it easy'? Don't give me that shit! My clothes are probably cheaper than yours! Fucking Asda jeans and t-shirt! You CHOOSE to wear tracksuits all the fucking time! And if you want to get all 'poor me' about going to prison, perhaps you shouldn't stab cunts with a screwdriver then!

Jake again braced himself for violence. This time he intended to just swing back and hope to connect before his poor cardio-vascular system failed him. He wanted to scream about the extra complications he had with being trapped in the same evening repeatedly, but considered it ultimately a moot point wasted on this cretin who wouldn't grasp the concept, anyway. He was shocked by the resigned tone that followed, however.

- When you're right, you're right. I've always had a problem with my temper. I hate getting embarrassed and people laughing at me. Been the same all my life. And I lash out. That time though, it was me against four guys though. They assumed I'd broken into one of their houses and started just leathering me whilst I was fixing Mam's front gate. I had a screwdriver in my hand and used it. When the coppers got involved they ignored my side of things. Four versus one, the one being me, a scrubby ratbag from the Nunny with ASBOS and stuff. I grew up with the wrong people and I struggle to get away from that. As for the trackies, I've owned them since I was a kid. I just don't put weight on.

- So you're the victim are you? No smoke without fire, chief.

- As a kid, I've been a dick. Like I said, I grew up with the wrong people. I try to get away from them and get new friends, but no-one wants to talk to me. You ever done anything you regret? Everyone has. Just some people make bigger mistakes.

Jake considered this. Derek had a point. He would change a lot of things about his past. Un-say things, not get involved with his exes. He wondered if he would be happier today if he'd never met them, or ended things earlier. Derek unwittingly opened a metaphysical can of worms in Jake's head which he continued to ponder as he carried on talking to Derek, aware that he'd more interest in what he had to say and mildly more empathetic to his situation.

- That why you hang round Matrix and The Barge? It didn't seem to be aimed at a person of your tastes.
- Yeah, but I've always liked metal and that. When I was a kid, I just kept it quiet. Nothing worse than being a Greebo on the Nunny. I dunno if my old mates pretended to like all that techno shit they used to put on, or they were the same.
- I can imagine. Bad enough being a Greebo on the Willows.

Jake remembered the times when he'd lived on another former council estate in Grimsby. Constantly enduring haranguing from people passing by, attacks on his house and threats of/ acts of violence simply because of his long hair and leather trench-coat. This made him fairly militant about what he perceived as the only legal and socially acceptable form of prejudice left. He realised over the years that all the other forms of bigotry still existed; racism, sexism and homophobia etc. Jake was aware that in terms of the need to end these forms of hatred, his particular sub-culture fell pretty far down on the list, although still not acceptable in his eyes, it wasn't a cause worthy enough to be championed until other intolerances had been eliminated. Derek interrupted his thoughts to talk about the Matrix.

- Thing is, I always saw the rock scene as being pretty friendly, yet people look at me and turn their nose up. I know I don't dress the part and I'm not as clever as other people, but don't I have a right to be included? I've seen you over the years at all of these places. I even went to one of your things once and loved the music, but people ignored me or looked at me like a piece of shit.
- Wait. So you know who I am. You've seen me around, yet when I pretended to be mentally ill earlier, you played along with it?
- I wasn't sure. You might have been in an accident like a mate I know. It's weird, I kind of knew and at one point it would make me mad but I remembered...

Derek trailed off. Jake remained curious as to why. He remembered the assault, seemingly so long ago, despite being the same evening, the anger was no longer as fresh in his mind as it could've been. But something about the way Derek stopped himself from talking after being so open and candid seemed off. He pressed.

- What do you mean you 'remembered'? Remembered what?

- Ah nothing. I remembered nothing, I'm just being daft.
- Let me put it this way, there is literally nothing you can say, short of being a nonce, that would give me a lesser opinion of you than I had before you walked up. It's a win for you and we are talking, which is kind of what you claimed to want in the first place yeah?
- Yeah. Not kind of. I saw you with your mates and a wanted the same thing, but I can't. It's mental.
- Right now, I'm living mental. Try me.

Derek exhaled and reached for another cigarette. He offered one to Jake and happy it got accepted. He tried to light his with no success and Jake leant over to assist. Derek was glad to have someone to talk to for once other than his immediate family and didn't want to ruin things by being an idiot. But he'd started, so needed to finish.

- C'mon Derek.
- It's strange. It's like a sort of dream, but not. I remember stuff now about tonight.
- You will find that's quite common. Most people remember things that happened in the previous few hours.
- Yeah, but it's different. It's like different things happened tonight and I'm having different memories. Like I can see how things are if I react a certain way. Thing is, these different things only involve you.

\-   Like what?

Jake trembled as Derek recounted different things he'd seen. He described the evening where Jake humiliated him in front of Sarah and how he'd reacted so violently, assuring Jake he held nothing but shame about that and how he'd died because of running away from the consequences. He continued to furnish Jake with more details most of which fell on ears closed off by deep contemplation. The main question that re-occurred in Jake's mind from various scenarios was this; does everyone possess multiple memories of the same evening?

Chapter 26.

Sarah stood outside the Matrix smoking as she pondered the facts Jim revealed about Jake's unfortunate experiences with women. She wondered what may have happened if they had tried to get together, something she had occasionally considered a possibility. She surprised herself as she imagined what the sex would be like, imagining a range of the almost perfect lover to a clumsy regrettable fumble. The images came with startling clarity which she almost considered that they actually happened.

But no, she thought, they didn't happen. That's stupid. It's just grief talking. Content with her rationalisation, she returned inside to hear more of Jim's telling of Jake's tale.

Chapter 27.

The rain continued to thrash the pavement outside the Grimsby Town hall. From the steps and the shelter from the porch, it seemed like a protective bubble. Jake almost imagined himself warm in its embrace. He had opted not to tell Derek what was going on with him, partially through a cruel desire for him to continue considering himself 'mental', but largely because he saw no purpose in revealing it, other than a lengthy explanation he couldn't be bothered with. Jake also considered until he had somehow made his friends and family understand, revealing his problems to a stranger he harboured a small amount of enmity towards would be a betrayal. Derek's eyes widened, anticipating some sort of explanation for his thoughts. Jake tried to oblige.

-   Sounds like you might be making progress then. If you are seeing consequences of your actions, then it means you are thinking before reacting.

Derek's face scrunched in distaste, happy to have a form of personal growth acknowledged, but un-satisfied with the answer, something appeared to be missing and made little sense, only he wasn't articulate enough to express it. Jake realised Derek didn't buy his rationalisation, Jake changed tack to distract Derek from the issue.

-   With everything you've said, I feel kind of guilty about the way I've thought of you. I knew nothing about you and I've been pretty judgemental towards you. For that I'm sorry. We all have a cross to bear, so I'll try to have a chat and stuff with you in the...

Jake hesitated for the briefest of seconds.

-   ... future.

As he said the words, Jake realised he actually meant it. He saw another option to the scenario with Sarah he'd never seen before. Derek wasn't being menacing. He was just a bit dim and didn't realise the concept of 'personal space'. Jake acknowledged a new option; to simply buy him a drink and talk to him, include him in the conversation. Derek beamed at Jake thankfully. Overjoyed someone he respected had acknowledged his presence with something other than contempt. Jake's distraction technique had worked and Derek no longer wondered about how the explanation about his 'memories' lacked substance.

-   Thanks. It really means a lot you listened.
-   Perhaps I should do that more often with people.

Derek continued to gush enthusiastically to Jake, but Jake grew distracted by the notion that maybe tonight was some cosmic form of Karma, an idea drummed into him watching Groundhog Day as a youth. Jake convinced himself because of the exchange with Derek, tonight would finally be over and wanted to celebrate.

- Tell you what, let's go get a couple back at the Barge.
- Yeah! I'm up for that!

As Jake and Derek braced the rain for the short walk back to The Barge, they chatted about music and films, almost like old friends. Jake still assumed Derek to be a bit of an idiot, but knew a person could never have too many friends and it was possible to help him stay calm in some situations, possibly even saving some poor sod from a kicking. Elated he looked forward to the end of his evening, going to sleep and the ordeal finally being over.

Jake was wrong. It was far from over.

Chapter 28.

-   Katie was an even bigger cunt than Clarice.

Craig, Sarah and Pete gathered back around the table, Jim remained eager to continue with his tale of Jake's past problems with the women in his life. Also pleased to note no-one seemed to be bored with him speaking. Or if they were, they hid it well, which seemed good enough for him.

-   I mean she's a straight up sociopath, no exaggeration. She flat out had no morals and seemed to do things for the sake of it. Remember that line from that film 'Everything coming out of her mouth is a lie and everything that goes in is a dick'? It totally applied to her. She lied almost constantly, even when she didn't need to. A thief too, she stole shit off loads of people, often for no reason.
-   Like what?

Pete interrupted Jim's flow as this became news to him. Also, he seemed to remember a few innocuous items he'd lost and wondered if it had anything to do with her.

-   Money from Jake for a start. He'd a bit of a windfall a few years back if you remember? Not life changing, but enough for a comfortable couple of years with no income. Anyway, being a generous guy and he would never object to helping out his girlfriend if she needed it, we saw that with Clarice. So all she needed to do was ask. Anyway, she basically watched him put his pin number in the cash machine and used to nick his card and get money out. Never a big amount, just a tenner here and there. Pointless as he would have given her it, anyway. He only realised later on when he checked back through his bank statements. He used to have this O.C.D. thing where he would only take cash out in multiples of fifty, so they weren't withdrawals made by him. When he finally realised, he confronted her about it and she tried denying it at first, then just said she got embarrassed asking him for money so like a lot of things with her, he let it go. But that wasn't the only thing. She got friendly with people he liked, then shit would go missing from their houses when she'd been round. She always denied it and Jake never found what had been stolen—never valuables, just irritating small shit. It certainly explained why in the two years or so he stayed with her, he never once met a single friend from her past. Which made him feel sorry for her with his massive Jesus complex. Ha! I forgot the time she nicked some lasses shoes!

Craig snorted drink through his nose laughing.

- Shoes?
- Yeah. Some old mate of Jake's missus got friendly with through work, a job HE got for Katie, by the way. Anyway,

the guy's missus invited Katie to her birthday thing and Jake didn't; he'd gone to an engagement party or some shit. Anyway, Katie shows up at the engagement party later on wearing some scabby Velcro trainers and told Jake this lass'd given them to her. Jake didn't think much of it other than it seemed gross wearing second hand shoes. They weren't new trainers, or expensive ones or anything like that. Two months passed by and this old mate gets in touch through someone else says his missus wants the money for the trainers she took! Jake was mortified, there was literally no reason for her to do it!

- Jesus! With all that, why did he even stay with her?

Sarah remained genuinely mystified by this. Jake had never been a person to mince words and would lay into people for far less. She couldn't imagine he would ever tolerate even the slightest amount of relationship crap, yet here she discovered he seemed like a doormat. Jim, happy to engage explained further.

- He had to put up with Clarice for around four years, constantly screaming at him, berating him, smacking him and accusing him of infidelity on an almost daily basis. An abusive relationship, the kind that would get a guy imprisoned if the roles reversed. Hell, perhaps if he'd reported her, she would have been. Anyway, Katie was the opposite of this. She never argued with him, in fact she never really made any demands of any type. Katie claimed to like everything he did and never asked him to do annoying stuff, like watch a film she liked that he didn't or anything. She also fed him a sob story about how her ex used to batter her and stuff, something in hindsight we figured to not be true in the slightest. Also, ever heard the saying 'crazy fucks the best'? It's true. And she apparently didn't have a gag reflex. But the combination of amazing sex, something Clarice denied him for too long and the fact that Katie was the opposite of her in terms of public arguments and constant screaming meant he reckoned he'd found the illustrious 'one'.

- I actually remember her coming in here a lot with him before and always thought there to be something 'off' about her. In all the years I've known Jake, I've never once seen him get violent apart from this one time he literally exploded at some guy, head-butted him a few times and mashed the guy's nose in. Looked awesome, by the way, Jakes hair sort of swallowing this guy's head and then releasing it looking like a bloody mess.

The table chuckled at the image Craig painted. Jim remained silent, slightly annoyed at the interruption, but intrigued as he wasn't there on this occasion and was unfamiliar with the story.

-   The bouncers tried to lob Jake out, but I stopped them. Like I said, never seen him like that before and gave him the benefit of the doubt. Turns out Katie told Jake the guy tried to drag her into the toilets saying he wanted to fuck her. No-one else seemed to see it and Jake saw the same guy earlier grab her arse and say something to her and told him it wasn't acceptable—obviously with liberal use of the words 'fuck' and 'cunt' to express it. Jake felt awful afterwards. He spent the rest of the night apologising and seemed shook up by how he'd been 'overtaken by rage', as he put it.

Jim considered this for a second.

-   With all that going on with them, it wouldn't have just been that situation causing it. It wasn't just the stealing with her, over time loads of stuff unravelled and he was basically on his guard all the time with her in the last year. He prided himself on being a fairly clever guy and she constantly would dupe him about shit—making him look stupid for falling for stuff time and time again. And that is one reason only I know about this, he'd got humiliated and wouldn't tell people how this seemingly dumb bitch got the better of him. The worst of it was when she fell pregnant.
-   Jake has a kid?

-   No. This shit very nearly broke him. I'd get a drink now, this will take a lot of explaining.

Pete grew angry. He'd never particularly liked Katie anyway, he also realised something wasn't quite right about her. Pete caught her one night pinning one of Jakes older friends up against the wall and kissing him and worked himself up trying to fathom how to let Jake know it happened. He remembered being worried Jake would somehow lash out at him in a 'shoot the messenger' type way, but he'd thanked him. Jake dismissed it as being a stupid drunken mistake and posited it wasn't the worst thing in the world when drunken snogs happen. He said he could easily let it slide, to the point where Pete was annoyed at how petty and trivial he'd made it seem, considering how much Pete dreaded telling him in the first place. Pete told Jake he didn't trust her and Jake responded that he was glad he had his brother looking out for him like that. Pride swelled and Pete was glad the protective brother bond worked both ways. He wasn't sure he wanted to listen to the rest of this tale, but couldn't tear himself away. Had he failed looking out for his brother? Sarah asked if Jake was father to a child and he realised there was still a lot they all didn't know about him. Pete wished he'd shared more, perhaps people may have been able to help.

Pete also grew more convinced, despite what others told him, Jake was still alive somewhere. He could not express how he knew, but he was certain. That certainty did not help with the helplessness that swelled his rage at Jake's exes. He remembered the pregnancy. What had happened?

Chapter 29.

- Where to mate?

The familiar question he'd heard too many times to signify the beginning of his seemingly never ending evening cut deeper than before. He'd been convinced that by becoming friendly with Scrobbo, now to only referred to as Derek, that he'd addressed some karmic balance. But this wasn't that case. 'Why haven't I jumped, Ziggy?', he thought sardonically.

As the evening continued, Jake doled out the insults, exchanged the pleasantries and let loose the quips he knew worked, but was distracted by his own morose musings. The only thing he changed; when Derek appeared in front of Sarah, he took over a few shots and began a friendly chat. This was the only part of the evening engaging him because of its relative novelty.

Jake finished the evening and silently climbed into bed, alone. He continued to do this for several months' worth of nights. Jake couldn't perceive a way out and ran out of ideas. He hadn't seen his family in so long. His friends, though he cared for them dearly, said nothing new and wouldn't understand his predicament.

Jake saw no alternative. He considered the only thing left for him to do.

- Where to mate?

Chapter 30.

- So, the pregnancy?

Pete tried to wrestle the conversation from the banal pleasantries that took over after buying drinks. Jim shared the same sentiment, irritated by how easily distracted people got. Confident people again paid attention thanks to Pete's urging, he pressed on.

- First, you all remember Billy? I know you don't Sarah, but he used to be one of Jake's best mates for a while. They used to spend loads of time together bollocking about and watching TV etc. Anyway, one night he'd gone out and caught Katie with her tongue down his throat. Jake was gutted. Billy scurried away, and he didn't know how to react. Katie sat there all blank-faced as Jake kept asking her questions she didn't answer and it frustrated him all the more. I told you she was a sociopath, yeah? It used to be one of her tricks when she did something fucked up, because she wasn't very clever, she used to let Jake argue himself tired and he would end up 'offering' scenarios, giving her an 'out'.
- What does that mean?
- Well, if he asked her why she'd done something, she just wouldn't respond, so he would ask her specifics; was it because of this or was it because of that? So she

eventually went along with the easiest option. He thought she'd some mental problem or other and the liberal loony in him kept trying to 'understand'. He read a lot on mental health conditions, personality disorders, etc. The answer had always been there; the cunt was a sociopath, but he would always look for a reason why it didn't apply to her, she never really showed any emotion, but when she did, it was the basest kind she reckoned appropriate for the situation.

- Ah. So he gave her a reason, and she simply agreed with it?

- Yeah. Anyway, he caught her copping off with his best mate. He ended up again putting it down to a drunken snog and not attributing anything to it, he didn't want to lose her and his best mate at the same time. He chatted with Billy and thought it had all blown over.

- The fuck has this got to do with the pregnancy?

- I'm getting to that, Pete. It's all sort of tied in. Anyway, she'd started seeing Billy behind his back for a while, so Billy told her he loved her too and stirred shit making out Jake didn't love her etc. Fucking childish cunt. Whilst this was going on, she told Jake they were pregnant. Jake was shocked at first, but then overjoyed. Gave himself bronchitis with the amount of cigars people bought him. He'd announced it to his family, friends, on Facebook and everything. What made it more important to him was she'd previously said she was unable to have kids. Another lie to bolster her 'damaged' image that made him forgive stupid shit.

- Yeah, I remember, didn't she have a miscarriage?

- Well. This is where the Billy shit came in. Billy sent her messages saying he loved her and stuff and for whatever reason, she showed Jake them. Probably the sick side of her wanting to see a reaction to the fucked up situation she'd created and encouraged. Things all kicked off and Jake started going fucking ballistic at this Billy guy, this all happening whilst Jake was at work. Katie soon told him about the 'miscarriage' and said she was headed to the hospital. Jake managed to get away from work an hour later to find her stood waiting outside, claiming she'd been seen to and the baby was gone. Jake was devastated by this and it served its purpose; it distracted him from the Billy situation where her encouragement had surfaced in back-and-forth messages that Billy sent him copies of. Jake put all this together through the overwhelming shit he had to deal with all at once, then boom! She tries to off herself.

- What?

- Yeah. Except she claimed to. They end up back at the hospital again. She claimed to have taken a load of pills and the doctors saw her privately and seemingly left her alone. She did her usual no speaking shit to him and he tried to talk to a nurse about it. He mentioned she'd been there earlier for a miscarriage and the nurse, breaking all sorts of confidentiality shit, said Katie hadn't been seen that day at all.

- So she was still pregnant?
- No. Jake was cunt-blind, but not stupid. He realised straight away she'd made the whole thing up. There was no pregnancy. She'd planned this from the start, probably choosing the day to show the messages from Billy as the same day she faked a miscarriage. I mean, it meant nothing to her, but real or not, in his mind, Jake lost a kid that day. Some mental health team got involved, but Jake couldn't bring himself to tell people what happened, how they'd all been duped like him. He felt stupid, angry, hurt. He'd lost his best friend, his fiancé, as they'd got engaged at that point, and a child in the space of a few hours. So he made a stupid decision. He stayed with her and kept it all a secret.
- Why?
- He still bought into the whole 'broken girl' routine and foolishly thought he could help. Plus, and perhaps most importantly, he wanted to ensure Billy got no happiness from her. I told him it seemed ridiculous, and he needed to get away, but he was determined to try to 'help' her and wipe Billy from his life. It lasted a few months. After

that, he began receiving private messages from his other cunt ex, Clarice, on a forum he used to go on.

Pete, incensed, wanted to find Katie and smash her face in. He'd also been upset by the miscarriage news, looking forward to being an uncle, and assumed Jake's 'I've decided I don't want any kids now' diatribes afterwards to be a result of grief. Pete wished he'd known at the time. He would have tried to force Jake to leave her, or at least, he would have tried.

Chapter 31.

Jake's bed lay unmade in his untidy room. Covers strewn back leaving space for the recently used laptop, screen still glowing illuminating the room. On the laptop Jake placed a sticky note stating 'Password: 420blaYzeit69'. His pirated copy of Word 2007 was open on a document titled 'To Pete family and friends'. The entire document written in Comic Sans font, detracting somewhat from the tone of the missive.

Everyone. I'm sorry about this, I really am. I didn't come to this decision lightly. Things in my life went from bad to worse. I stopped doing what I loved for a living due to circumstances beyond my control. I then had to take a job I detested and had to stay because there was simply nothing else around, which I'm now losing. The two relationships I've had in the last ten years took an irreplaceable chunk from me I will never get back. More to the point, I won't be able to trust anyone in the same way again, short of my family and friends. You've all been the one shining light in my life and I want every one of you to understand that none of you failed in any way. This is all on me. I'm weak. I wish I possessed the same strength you all seem to in being able to cope with what this shitty life throws our way.

No-one will believe what is happening to me at the moment, but I assure you it is true. I've been trapped in the same evening over and over again for god knows how long now, I haven't been keeping track. I tried riding it out for as long as I could stand, hoping that something would change. No idea why it happened or how it happened, but most importantly, I can't find a way out. It's like Groundhog Day, but there is no Bill Murray, no face full of pathos whilst waving goodbye in the path of a train. This is the only end to the culmination of all the crap that preceded it. The one constant in my life has been all of you, yet this situation is taking that away from me too. It's like I'm watching a video of the same evening over and over again, I'm continuing against all odds whilst everything else seems like a vivid memory. I realise how unbelievable this sounds and questioned my sanity several times. But it's real. Too fucking real.

So I'm out. Again, I want to stress, there was nothing you could've done to stop this and I wouldn't be ending it all if I weren't trapped. I wouldn't ever do this to any of you in the past, despite considering it, because you all mean so much to me. I've carried on for as long as I can cope with, but without an end in sight and no life to look forward to beyond it, I can't anymore. I don't even know if I still exist 'tomorrow' anyway, or if I've gone missing. At least this way, I see that you will have answers, rather than worry, need to search or blame yourselves.

I love you all, you made my life worth living. This doesn't fall on any of you.

Jake.

The power savings on the laptop caused the screen to fade. The room became dark.

Chapter 32.

- Anyway, Clarice started messaging Jake on that old forum we used to post on.

As much as he'd enjoyed holding court telling the stories about Jake and his unsuccessful love life, Jim got bored. The alcohol made the surrounding people and raucousness an inviting distraction he ached to get involved with. He also felt a sadness telling people who'd been previously unaware the details, noting Pete visibly shaken by some of his revelations. It wasn't his intention to upset people, but to demonstrate Jake possessed a lot more strength than people gave him credit for and to excuse some of his less than savoury interactions in the past. Jim also had pride that Jake considered him a confidante. He didn't mourn however, he'd an overwhelming sense Jake was still alive, for reasons he couldn't pinpoint.

- Jake saw she'd recently posted on there. Innocuous stuff really, never directly interacting with any of his posts, but general chit-chat; bands she'd been listening to, TV shows and films she'd enjoyed and that sort of shit. It wound him up. He knew her well, and all the things she claimed she now liked were things she'd dismissed as 'shit' years earlier. Another reason it was a toxic relationship— everything he ever loved was 'shit' to her. Anyway, she said she'd be going to some event or other and Jake got anxious, because he would be at the same thing with Katie. He hadn't seen her in three years and didn't want to see her either, so planned on not going. But I talked him round. "Fuck that cow," I said she isn't going to ruin my mate's nights at a whim. She never showed anyway, but it ended up distracting him as he constantly watched the door, worried about an inevitable public embarrassment or her possibly starting on his fiancé. She was never shy about kicking off with other women if they so much as looked in his direction.

- I thought you said she messaged him personally?

- Yeah, I'm getting to it. Around the same time, Katie had been 'working' in a factory and he was on the bones of his arse, barely able to make rent and bills and so on. The job was only part time, but essential as it meant they could eat and have hot water, basics, y'know? Anyway, she must have lost the job or something, but pretended to go to work every day for like five or six weeks. At the same time, she stole his bank details and applied for payday loans in his name, took his card whilst he slept, withdrew the money and gave it back to him, not telling him it would come out of his account later with massive interest. When she couldn't get loans anymore, she came to him empty handed on payday, which caused a row, then when the idiot loans took their money from his account, he has a lengthy discussion with the bank, he realised what happened, he rang her and she didn't answer. He got home, and she'd gone. Her stuff all still there, she'd fucked off. After two days of him frantically trying to find her, she finally messaged him back saying she'd tried to top herself again and stayed in a hostel in another town.

- Shit. But what does it have to do with Clarice?

- That's when he got private messages off her. Saying shit like 'I've spilt up with my boyfriend, I miss you and can we try again? Jake ignored them as he was stupidly still in love with Katie and wanted to 'help' her. Katie kept e-mailing him telling him she'd been getting 'crisis counselling'—something which another mutual friend had recently been getting so her descriptions made sense. It was all bullshit, yet again. He kept getting messages from Clarice and he checked the IP address. Turns out they were all posted from a public library in Grimsby and Jake knew Clarice didn't live round here anymore and hadn't for years. He sent a reply saying 'Katie, I thought you're getting help?' They stopped after he sent that message. Katie had been posting as Clarice for about two months, creating an 'identity' to again distract Jake from what she was actually doing, the fucking sociopath. Anyway, he e-mailed Katie again, telling her to stop with the stupid games and to be honest with him. She came back the next week, and they apparently held a long talk, he said he needed to know if she wasn't working so he could plan ahead, and if necessary, put off paying the bills in favour of buying food. She said she hadn't been happy with what a dead end she was in and wanted to push forward to do something else, go to university or something. Jake encouraged her too and like an idiot, believed her. When she left in the morning to get her stuff from the 'hostel', he thought the worst was behind him. She texted him ten minutes later saying 'I love you, I miss you already'. That was the last he ever heard from her. She'd stolen a tenner out of his wallet and his Nintendo DS. She left all of her clothes and everything. He tried contacting her for months, she never responded. It was during her leaving he got his job at the DWP and was able to pay stuff off, live comfortably for a change. The whole thing just destroyed him though. He stopped simply getting pissed on a night out and attacked booze like crazy. He got blackout drunk, and I had loads of calls from him at four or five in the morning switching between him raging and breaking down sobbing for an hour at a time. Between Clarice and Katie, he lost all ability to trust people. He only perceived potential problems with anyone new he met, so kept everyone at a distance. And he blamed himself. I kept on telling him it wasn't his fault, but he insisted that if he'd dealt with things better, he may have prevented it, or he somehow deserved it because he considered himself a shitty person. He wouldn't be convinced otherwise, and it never changed, he is still the same way to this day.

-   Was. To THAT day.

Pete's eyes glazed with tears threatening to erupt as he clenched his fists under the table. He was hurt and angry, not at Jake or Jim, but that his brother had to go through this without help. He felt impotent and wanted revenge. Natasha spotted his glowering from the bar and bought a round of shots. Natasha took them over to the table, she proposed a toast to Jake's memory. Everyone accepted and slowly filtered away to mingle with the rest of the club, drinking heavily keeping Chloe rushed off her feet and away from the call of her social media accounts. It's what Jake would have wanted.

Chapter 33.

Jake sidled along the edge of the car park at the DWP building where he used to work. He did so to avoid setting off the security lights at the side as he didn't want to be prevented from undertaking his final plan. The large wrought iron gates that closed in the car park were unlocked, which was a relief as he wasn't sure his bulky frame would make the climb over.

He reached the back entrance to the drab building, cursing as he scraped the back of his hand against the pebble-dashing on the walls as he reached to put in the security code to enter the building. Jake was shocked to discover it hadn't changed, but then reasoned, 'why would it?'

He walked through the door into the main foyer and noticed one lift activate. 'Shit', he thought, he realised there were security staff in the building at night. He pushed through the spring loaded doors to the fire escape and pushed them closed gently, to prevent a thud. Stealthily, he crept up the stairs, trying to keep aware of any noises that would betray a security guards presence. After two floors, his confidence he would achieve his goal grew, but he was fatigued by the climb. Five more floors to go.

He froze as he heard the guard opening the door on the ground floor and prayed to a deity he didn't believe in that the guard wouldn't pursue.

- No one here. Must be a glitch or something.
- Ok. I'll check the stairwell just in case.

Jake swore inwardly as he silently opened the fire doors leading to the floor three lobby. He hid behind the lift shaft peering at the door he'd entered through for what seemed like an eternity. He saw a beam of light waving from the upper floor and was relieved that what the second guard meant by 'checking the stairs' was simply to poke his head through the door and wave his torch about. Jake waited for an acceptable amount of time, then continued his trek up the fire escape stairs to the final roofed area of the building.

As he reached the door to the roof entrance, he was confronted by another security panel, its existence previously unknown to him. He paused and considered that this would alert the guards a second time, this time they would be more vigilant and possibly stop him. As he rested his hand on the door to the roof, it moved forward sending him almost tumbling out to the cold wet February air. He thanked again the lacklustre security of the building and strode with purpose to the edge and peered over.

As he did so, he felt the familiar giddy and nauseous sensation that happened whenever he was at height. He had always been phobic of being high up, to the point where he was unable to watch footage at an altitude on TV. He considered that this wasn't the best choice of his final moments and steeled himself to look again. His legs trembled, and he backed away, resting against the wall of the doorway entrance to psyche himself up for the last push. Once again he crept closer to the small wall surrounding the edge of the building and peered over, trying to force his fear away. It didn't work. The tightness in his chest made him take panicked gasps as breaths and his legs almost buckled as he back again to the brick wall central to the rooftop, scraping the back of his hand against the coarse bricks as he did so.

Jake slumped down against the doorway. He thought about the final words he left on his laptop at home. How he could have done better. At the time of writing, he had been typing through racking sobs and had cut his thoughts short. Perhaps he hadn't been as explicit as possible about how much everyone meant to him? He needed to say more, to make certain that people knew the predicament he was in and how this was the only way. He stared accusingly at the two foot high wall surrounding the building. A swift jog and a vault and it would be an end to this nightmare.

He stood up again and looked around at the area. With the industrial areas lit up and the waters still, the goods inwards area of the docks had a postcard like look to them. He admired the view, a rare glimpse of beauty in a town he considered so ugly. It was after 3am, so traffic was almost non-existent, Freeman Street, once a hive of commerce in the town in the 80s, now a shell of its former self with a myriad of stores' barriers shut permanently. The street had become synonymous with scratters and feckless dregs, yet now was silent. At night it wasn't a reminder of a town failed by its country, but one of possibility for the future.

Jake paused. Had he tried everything? Did he need to end it all tonight? Now more than ever he needed to speak to someone else about things–but even if they believed him, who knew anything about this situation? He needed to talk with Jim, he had often reasoned things out with him in the past and hoped that somehow he could figure out at least a thread for him to pull on.

Realising that getting out of the building would be as much as a ball-ache as getting in, Jake once again slumped against the doorway of the building. He soaked in the rare calming silence of Grimsby, he wrapped the long leather coat tightly around himself as the chill bit. With the silence and the comfort of his own body heat, Jake soon drifted into sleep.

-   Where to mate?

Chapter 34.

Jim stared at his reflection in the mirror. Pleased his hangover to be so minor, it was almost nothing, since his role as storyteller the previous evening had prevented him from drinking as heavily as he might, he considered he should try that more often. A night out in Grimsby became a race to oblivion to mask that it either wasn't as good as it used to be, or he'd become too old to appreciate it.

He gazed at the straggly hair he'd defiantly kept around the sides of his head after baldness spread outwards from the top. The previous evening he overheard someone refer to him as 'egg-in-nest' and it bothered him. He knew he looked ridiculous, and he had finally had enough. Jim reached for his clippers, usually only used for trimming his unruly pubic region, he set them to the sides of his head. He worked diligently to ensure he got as much as was visible, switching to a razor to remove traces of hair from his scalp. With the lack of an extra mirror, he proved surprisingly efficient and grew impressed with the results.

Next to go would be his beard. Trimming it down to a small goatee surrounding his mouth, he briefly regretted his decision when his double chin became much more visible, but upon more inspection, it wasn't so bad. He appeared lighter. The Hulk Hogan comparisons and such-like would now stop and now people had to consider him a person, rather than just some funny looking guy. Who knows? Maybe a relationship would spring from his new visage? He theorised women liked men trying to improve themselves. He took a selfie and immediately posted it to Facebook with the caption 'new look, a new me'. Six likes within seconds.

He went downstairs, remembering he'd agreed to meet Sarah and Pete at Riverhead Coffee in town and skipped breakfast. Jim had resolved to stop being late for arrangements with people, so he rushed to his car. He selected Fear Factory from his now ancient multi-changer stereo and cranked up the volume, his speakers blasting out his favourite 'Edgecrusher' and he nodded his head in appreciation to the music in the short journey. His head felt cold, so he grabbed his old black hat from the back of his car and put it on. His mood good, for perhaps the first time in a long time. He checked his phone again; twenty-one likes and five comments. He beamed and looked forward to his friends' reactions when he walked in to meet them.

He ordered a salted caramel macchiato, or 'twatachino' as Jake used to call it and walked up the stairs of the coffee shop they all frequented, anticipating the compliments he was about to receive for his new image. At first they didn't notice him, so he stood over them until they turned to face him. Pete erupted in laughter and Sarah covered her mouth to hide a smirk. Pete, through giggles spluttered out one sentence before laughing uproariously and triggering Sarah to join him.

- I guess you are the one who knocks, Heisenberg!

Jim thought, 'my friends are bastards'.

Chapter 35.

- Can't we stay here for a bit?

Jim protested Jake's insistence they leave the Matrix 'for a word'. He wanted no heavy conversation, focussed as he was on imbibing as much alcohol as possible in what he saw as a short space of time. The look on Jake's face was one of desperation and after a half an hour of belligerent refusal, Jim relented and followed Jake to the area affectionately known amongst their circles as 'Skutter Roof'. As they walked through the large black gates opening the club, Jake mumbled a greeting to Derek as they passed, who smiled in acknowledgment. Jim flashed Jake a confused glance.

Through a piss-smelling alleyway between two buildings opposite the Matrix club, they emerged into a small carpark used by the legal offices nearby. A wrought-iron stairwell led to a fire escape area for the offices, strewn with empty cans and bottles, some of which at least five years old. The area was where many of their circle of friends used for 'skutter drinking', the act of drinking cheap booze to make an evening cost less, often comprising 'comedy' drinks such as Lambrini, Scotsmac and Foxhunter. Anything they may have imagined being the drink of choice for tramps, was consumed in this area, weather permitting.

The context for Jake and Jim's sojourn to their old stamping ground proved far less jovial. Jake needed Jim's attention with no distractions. It would be hard enough to convince him of his situation without the added annoyance of stopping every few minutes to respond to inane chatter.

- So what's so important you have to drag us away from valuable drinking time? I've barely got a buzz yet!
- I needed you relatively sober dude. I need your help and I need you to realise how serious I am and how I'm not making this up.
- So what is it?
- Best to rip off the plaster... I'm trapped in the same evening over and over again.
- Ohhhh. Yeah, I feel that way too. Grimsby has got stale definitely. Same fucking faces, same fucking songs...
- No! Not metaphorically. Literally. What happens is I keep living this same February evening repeatedly, then if I go to sleep or lose consciousness, I'm back in the taxi with the driver asking 'where to mate?' Even if you don't believe me, play devil's advocate and just humour me.

Jim considered what he was being told. His initial reaction was that Jake talked bullshit, but the serious nature of his tone and demeanour gave him pause. As a sci-fi fan, he had often wondered if there was any factual basis to a lot of different tales within the oeuvre. At the very least, it seemed an interesting premise and one he wanted to hear more about.

- Go on.
- You reckon I'm telling the truth?
- I'm not sure. You don't seem like you're joking, so either it's true or you're having a breakdown. If I can help any way, I will

Jake became glad of Jim not making an issue out of how fantastic his predicament was and felt a surge of love for his friend. He spent the following hour explaining in detail as much of the events as he could remember. Jim simply nodded and more things seemed to make sense, particularly Jake's acknowledgement of Scrobbo as they left the Matrix. As they talked, the rain began and Jim suggested they go back to the sheltered area of the Matrix's smoking section. He needed a drink. Jake then dropped the bombshell as they stood in the relative quiet of the smoking area, no-one else around due to the weather.

- So that leads me to last night. Which I intended to be my last night. I left a note on my laptop and snuck into the DWP building to throw myself off the roof.
- What the fuck! Why? Did you do it? Did you consider the rest of us? That's fucking shitty. Jesus. Don't. That's all I'm saying, we can try to figure it out.

- I've had enough man. I want to get out of it. It's like this is all my life is now. I didn't do it, obviously. This isn't a comedy. I'm pretty sure death will be the end. I did and do think about the rest of you. That's a huge factor, one that kept me going for far longer than I could have before. But also, I dunno what happens tomorrow. I dunno if I'm around, if I've gone missing or what. It messes with my head. I know this though, people are having different memories of this evening. Later you will remember stuff you assumed happened on a different night, or will put down to being imagination as it isn't as 'strong' as others. Try to 'remember' tonight and the stuff that has happened. Anything different?

Jim cast his mind back over the previous few hours and realised Jake was correct. He tried to recall different events.

- That bird had a row with you... Scrobbo kicked fuck out of you? Did those things happen?
- Yes. I left those out deliberately as I hoped you might 'remember' them.
- Yeah, it's really weird though. It's fuzzy, I keep thinking I imagined it all, y'know like when you dwell on situations in your past and how they could have gone differently, or you've said the 'right' thing?
- Derek clued me into that. Had a long chat with him one night.

- Scrobbo? After he kicked fuck out of you?
- Yeah, I tried to goad him into doing it again. For some reason, he didn't try to rationalise the different memories and just accepted them.
- Probably cos he is thick as fuck.
- It doesn't matter. He helped me suss this aspect out. So I'm thankful to him. He also made me realise that we had been cunts to him a bit too.
- Hippy.
- Maybe. Thing is, I saw a different way out of situation I only saw two different options to before. Anyway. It doesn't change how stuck I am. I only know about time stuff from films, which are all bollocks. I do not understand theoretical physics or anything. What can we do? Bear in mind, I have to explain all of this to you again tomorrow-slash-tonight.

Jim drained his Desperado and pondered whilst Jake talked. As he said 'physics', he excitedly came up with an idea.

- Terry! Scotch Terry!
- What?
- He was like a physics genius or something before he knocked up that bird and became a pisshead!
- Yeah?

-   Yeah, he always started wibbling on about it when he would get pissy at the end of a night! Go see him! If anyone knows, he will!

Jake had a sliver of hope once again. It was too late to visit this evening, but he would definitely do that in his version of tomorrow. Jim wanted to continue talking about his quagmire and Jake found himself happy to oblige, thankful for once for the change in conversation. As Jake bought another drink and returned, Jim asked with a grin;

-   Did you play the lottery?

Chapter 36.

Derek walked out of the Jobcentre in a temper. He sensed signs of his old habits returning borne out of impotence and frustration at his situation. He'd been shifted onto a new advisor who snottily implied that the reason he hadn't found work to be purely down to his own failings and not his prison spell. Derek knew he wasn't a clever man, but he also was aware a spell at Her Majesty's Pleasure severely narrowed his employment options.

The advisor recommended he applies for an apprenticeship for two-pound-fifty an hour and that he omit the fact he'd already previously gone through an apprenticeship as a mechanic in his youth, Derek thought this sounded wrong, yet unable to put it into words, made further difficult by the advisor constantly talking over him. His opinions clearly not wanted or valued in the slightest.

Derek tried working through an agency at one of the local factories. This was fine for a week, then he turned up for work at 6am daily and told often he wasn't required, along with many others. The resulting fluctuating income, lucky if he worked a full shift in a week, caused no amount of headaches sorting out hours with the Jobcentre. He'd been sanctioned during this time for failure to attend an appointment when he was at work, despite trying to ring in to inform them on his break times, only to be met with lengthy call queues that ate his entire fifteen minutes. After a full week of being sent home, he decided not to go again as it wasn't worth it to him.

Derek crossed the busy road of Victoria Street and headed towards Tesco. He wanted a treat and decided to have a cup of tea and a cake in the store cafeteria. This would often be as sophisticated as Derek ever got, he got self-conscious doing this as he perceived it as too 'posh' for him. As he slurped his tea, he garnered a few looks from other patrons as he chewed his cake with his mouth open, lost in thought.

He remembered one of his encounters with Jake, the time they held a long conversation, where he discovered what was going on and since then, on the same night, they drank together on a few occasions. Derek realised the way people perceived him was often a problem, he'd tried to make some positive changes. Gone were the ancient tracksuits replaced by cheap supermarket jeans and t-shirts, something he'd been amassing over several weeks. He grew his hair a little, no longer sporting the shorn head that made him look like he grew up plagued by nits, which he did. Derek noticed he no longer elicited sneers from passers-by, in fact they tended to not notice him, which he preferred.

He also tried to restrain his emotions, not wanting to lash out at people because it had negative consequences. Dying had a profound impact on him in this regard. It must be rare for people to remember their own deaths. Nikki Sixx out of Motley Crue maybe, but that was about it. He'd tried to attend the memorial service for Jake at the Matrix club, wanting to inform people that Jake was ok, but he'd been refused entry at the door. The old version of him would have caused a scene and threatened violence, or actually committed it. They lacked the knowledge he did about the entire bizarre scenario, so he exercised his newly found reasoning skills and walked away, feeling good about the fact he could do so.

He hoped Jake would come back soon. Despite their initial enmity and relatively short amount of time spent together, Derek viewed him as a positive influence and a friend. With genuine friends being in short supply for Derek, it made Jake more important in his eyes.

He knew he couldn't help Jake out of the time-loop, but he could try again to assure his friends and family he isn't dead. How or when to do this was something that plagued him for weeks. He left the café, taking his cup and plate over to the counter which caused him to receive a beaming smile from a member of staff. His enforced prison etiquette coming across as good manners in this situation.

He continued down Victoria Street, heading into Grimsby town centre. Across the road he spotted Jake's good friend, the one he thought looked like a clever wrestler, except now he'd cut all of his hair and most of his beard off and wore a hat. Derek looked at this as an opportunity and followed him until he walked into Riverhead Coffee. Courage failing him, it was hard enough to approach these people with a story so out there, it was unbelievable, but to do it in a place he saw as so highbrow, it excluded him entry was almost too much.

Steeling himself, he walked inside and watched Jake's friend go upstairs. He ordered a coffee and took nervous steps to follow.

Chapter 37.

- Where to mate?

Jake barked out the street name where he remembered his old friend of sorts lived. He wasn't sure which number, and if honest with himself, he wasn't sure which one to look for either. He held a vague idea, having only been there when utterly shit-faced, so he resolved to knock on doors until he found the right one. The taxi driver tutted at his vague directions, but dutifully set off.

Jake rarely visited the East Marsh side of town apart from to travel nearby to get to work. It reminded him of the many women he'd seen over the years that failed to let go of their youth. There was no doubt that the area had once been attractive, perhaps sought after even, but now time and poverty ravaged it, some houses worse than others. Many lacked gardens, their front doors opening straight onto the pavement, but he seemed to recall Scotch Terry having a front yard as he was sure he fell over his wall one night after his housewarming party. He never considered it possible to 'downgrade' from living on the Willows Estate, but Terry found a way.

The taxi turned into the street that seemed familiar, he strained to see if he recognised any of the buildings to no avail. Until he spotted a garden containing a rusty old washing machine and grass growing higher than the wall that surrounded it. The wall also had bricks missing from the top as if something heavy banged into it.

- Just here mate.

Jake paid the driver and braced himself for the awkwardness he would get asking a person for help he'd largely fell out of contact with. He remembered Terry was pissed off at him for some reason, but drew a blank as to why. He knocked with trepidation on the peeling green paint of the wooden front door. The panels appeared to be rotten, but he reasoned that any burglars wouldn't bother since the outside appearance was that of a household that held nothing worth stealing.

Terry opened the door and gazed at Jake; a flash of both anger and confusion behind his eyes.

- Whit is it yir wantin?
- In a nutshell Terry, I need your help. Can I come in? It's a bit complicated to explain.

Terry paused, savouring the anxiety as he held off on his reply. He would let Jake in, curiosity already dictated this, but he wanted to relish the brief power he had. He nodded inside and disappeared down the hall into his living room. Jake followed and wrinkled his nose in distaste at the smell of ten thousand cigarettes and mounting takeaway containers. He noticed a glass half-empty with whisky on the sideboard next to a well-worn armchair and counted at least five ashtrays, overflowing with tab-ends and roll-ups. He sat down on the three seater sofa opposite Terry, avoiding a stain he largely suspected to be dried semen.

- So. Spit it oot. Whit's wrang?
- First, are you pissed off at me? I've not seen you in a while and get the impression I did something last time we got leathered that fucked you off.
- Well think back Jakey-boy. Whit wis the last time we wir drinking?

Jake paused and remembered the 'sobriety intervention' with a sinking realisation. Terry noticed this and cackled.

- So ye remember, aye? Ah'd been sober fir a wee while til yous lot came roond and shattered that yin.
- You're an alcoholic?
- Ye never knew?
- I just assumed you were in the same boat as us, needing to get battered a lot. I never fathomed you were, like, dependent on it. Seriously man, do you reckon I'd have done that? We assumed we hadn't seen you in a while because you were down in the dumps. Honestly man, I'm sorry. Have you not been able to stop again since?

Terry shook his head slowly, but rested back in his chair. Jake was a cunt, but wasn't malicious in that way. He liked the fact he'd made him feel guilty, but now regretted he'd done so.

Apart from the piss-taking, he'd enjoyed Jake's company on a superficial level and was miffed that he saw no-one after he'd stopped going out. Until now.

- Mebbee a bit pissed aff at mysel' aye? Yir right, you weren't tae realise. Ah nivir told any of yis. But yir no stupid, ye could have figured it out, well!
- It makes sense now, yeah. Wood for the trees though. How do you spot an alkie in a sea of piss-heads?
- Ah dinnae ken, how de ye spot an alkie in a sea ay pish-heids?
- It wasn't a joke man. I made a point with a rhetorical question.

Again, his bollocks-speak made him look foolish. Terry snapped back at Jake.

- So tell me why yir fuckin' here!

Jake started slowly and explained his circumstances, with the now pre-requisite 'I know this is unbelievable, but...' to begin. To his shock, Terry needed little convincing and grew increasingly animated as he continued to talk. He chuckled at the stories about the girl in the dressing gown and the short sighted way he dealt with Scrobbo. He asked Jake with a puzzled grin why he came to him for help.

- Because you're some sort of physics prodigy.

Terry flattered that Jake was aware of his credentials even though Jake only found this out through conversation with Jim. Noting that Terry seemed pleased with the acknowledgment, he chose not to share this particular nugget of information.

- So you believe me?
- Ah'm no sure. I kin see YOU believe it. It's fuckin' oot thir and nae mistake.
- Do you know a way out?
- Ah'll try tae come up wi' something as the night goes on.

Terry picked up his half-full tumbler of whiskey and was about to take a sip, when he remembered something he'd read a few years back and put it down again with excitement. He didn't touch the glass again for the rest of the evening.

Chapter 38.

-   You're Jake's mate yeah?

As an opening line to a conversation, it lacked subtlety, but Derek was too nervous to even consider usual social protocols, not that he was particularly au fait with them as is. Jim nodded, curious as to the point of the conversation.

-   And you're his brother?

Pete glared at Derek, unaware of who he was and why he spoke about his missing brother.

-   And you're his girlfriend?
-   I'm his friend that is a girl, yes.

Derek was lost as to how to continue the conversation at this point. He didn't understand the best way to touch on what he wanted to say. He sat down to the bemused faces around him and slurped the excess coffee from his saucer as he struggled to come up with the right words. Jim became irritated with what he saw as a theatrical pause before getting to the point.

-   Well, that's who we are. Who the fuck are you?
-   Derek

Jim's eye's bulged incredulously as if to suggest he expand on the revelation his name seemed to suggest. His cue was not taken up on, however. Jim continued in an angrier tone.

- And who in the suffering fuck is Derek?
- It's me...
- Jesus! I got that bit. Who. The. Fuck. Are. You?

Derek sighed wearily as he realised the three people did not recognise him although glad at the same time because it proved his positive changes to be working. He reluctantly expanded on his identity.

- Scrobbo. People called me Scrobbo. I hated it.
- Eh? You don't look like him.
- I don't want to. But it's me. I need to say something.

Pete continued to glare at Derek. Jim tensed up at the mention of his name, he remembered who he was and didn't like the fact he sat here. Sarah looked confused.

- So Derek... what do you want to say. Bit sick of the dramatics. Just spit it out or fuck off.
- It's Jake... he's ok. He is alive but...
- FUCK YOU!!!!

Pete roared as he launched himself across the table at Derek. They both tumbled to the dry hardwood floor of the quiet area of the coffee shop. Derek had spilled the coffee over the groin of his jeans and gasped in pain as he tried to pull the hot denim away from his balls. A brief pang of relief hit for a split second before Pete's fist slammed solidly into his ear, causing it to pop inside. A flurry of fists followed and Jim stood up to separate them, holding on for a few seconds to allow Pete to get a few shots in on Derek's jaw. Satisfied, he dragged the struggling Pete away, who still screamed at Derek.

- Fuck you! You reckon this is funny? You chavvy cunt! Fucking...
- Pete! Stop a minute! Not here at least.
- I expected this.

Derek forlornly cupped his scalded genitals and looked with pleading eyes at Pete. Jim took note that the supposedly violent Scrobbo had simply sat back and allowed the fracas to happen. Pete twitched angrily as Sarah looked on aghast.

- I wasn't joking. Not trying to wind you up. I know what has happened. You need to as well because you care about him. I'm sorry it has to come from someone like me.

Sarah felt a pang of empathy as Derek continued to talk in a dejected tone. Pete lurched forward again, but she touched his arm and shook her head.

- Let him speak.
- Thanks. I can't explain it proper. But remember the night he went missing. You all have different memories from that night, probably ones you often assume you imagined. I realised it on the same night. Had a long chat with Jake about it.

- Jake wouldn't talk to the likes of you scratter cunt!
- Pete! Pack it in and sit down!

Jim tried to recall as Derek suggested, Sarah did and as she realised, tears welled up in her eyes.

- You kicked the shit out of him. You died. He pretended to be disabled. Oh!

Sarah covered her mouth not wanting to say out loud about the other memories she had from the evening. The hurt glance Jake gave as he left her flat. His eyes, reddened, gazing at her as if saying goodbye for the final time. Pete looked at Sarah with concern and remembered his own experience that night. It proved more difficult for Pete since the only interaction he had happened over the telephone. He sat in silence contemplating the myriad of conversations he assumed to be a product of guilt. Jim broke the silence with what he thought was a revelation.

- Jake's trapped in a time loop type deal.
- Yes. That's it.
- He told me one time. Everything happens over and over again. So it sort of leaves echoes in our minds. But how can you remember it clear enough to talk to him about it Scr... Derek?
- Because I'm thick. Or at least that's how Jake put it.

Pete realised from this, Derek told the truth. Jim continued.

- Jake has told me this more than once.
- Ok, so we all clearly agree.
- I was so nasty to him once. He was telling me the truth!
- Snap out of it Sarah!
- So Jim, he's told you. Actually, come to think of it, he told me too. Fuck. But he's ok? What do we do?

Derek looked at Pete dejectedly.

- He is ok. As much as you can be I guess. As for what anyone can do? I dunno. I had to tell you guys he wasn't dead because people think he is. That's all I can do.

Derek stood up, wincing a little as he did so and turned to the dark corridor leading to the exit stairs. Pete, now released from Jim's clutches put a hand on his shoulder.

- Wait!
- What?
- You want another coffee? We spilt yours, plus if you walk out like that, it looks like you've pissed yourself. Dry off a bit.

Derek smiled and nodded. He picked up his chair and sat back down. Pete looked down at him with gratitude.

- And thanks. For letting us all know. Even I'd given up.
- Yeah, thanks man.

Sarah smiled to support Pete and Jim's sentiments as Derek looked embarrassed. Jim considered what options they have moving forward and drew a conclusion.

- I've got a weird notion, so it's probably an accurate recollection, I've said this before, but we need to see Scotch Terry!

Pete had a surge of hope he'd assumed all but gone. Jim was right. He had said it before. But as a sign, it must be a good thing, right?

Chapter 39

- Y'see, ah rid on some daft wee website a long time ago aboot some gadge that claimed to hae been in the same boat as you, son. Ah nivir considered it a possibility it was true until you posed the same kind ay thing.

Jake leaned in, intrigued that Terry may have a solution to his problem. Hope had again reared its head in his mind and a surge of gratitude was already coursing through his body.

- How did he get out of it?
- Well, he didnae. He affed himsel' But he left a note an' someone wrote aboot it on one ay these conspiracy websites where nutters talk shite aboot the government knowing and so on. Thir fuckin' hilarious. Ah minds ay this yin because ay the fact it made me contemplate the possibilities. There's like two kind ay physics—the established rules which always remain the same...
- Ye cannae change them?

Terry glared at Jake who was grinning mischievously at his own wit.

- Ye still wantin' muh help y'smart cunt?
- Yeah, sorry man. I couldn't resist it... you have to admit it was funny.

- I dinnae have to admit shite. Anyway. The other kind of physics is yir theoretical side, stuff like String Theory, stuff that hus'ne or can't be proven–yet. This is like a third kind which some folks call 'unexplained science'. Ghosts, magic and shite like that. May or may no' be true, but if it is, we have nae clue as tae the reasons behind it. A guy comes up wi' that? He gets fucking NAMED. Or at least in the world of science. Most cunts will nivir hear of them. Anyway... if I figure it oot... I get named. So ah'll help.
- How are you going to help?
- By thinking, that's all ah can dae.

Terry spent the rest of the evening quizzing Jake on the minutiae of what had happened to him, trying to puzzle an idea together. Still, he didn't touch his drink, so lost in possibilities, preferring to drink the frequent cups of tea Jake brought through from the kitchen. He noticed Jake was getting tired, so made two coffees, Jake's having extra spoons of coffee added to prolong the evening, which Terry was enjoying. Not only was his life's passion being brought to the forefront, but the tension had eased and he'd seen Jake in a different light, no longer a malevolent millstone around his neck, but as a buoy, rescuing him from drowning. Jake was not aware of these feelings. After handing Jake the loaded coffee he had his 'eureka' moment.

- Finally! Ah've hud an idea!
- Yeah?

-   If it doesnae work, we'll huv tae go through all this again, but ye kin tell me this earlier on so ah kin eliminate it, and mebbee bring us closer tae an answer.
-   Ok. Anything. I'm out of ideas.
-   You need tae stay awake.
-   I've tried that. It doesn't work. I told you, literally a split second nod-off sends me back.
-   Aye, that's muh point. You being trapped is kinda tied tae yir consciousness. Time is like elastic according tae some theories. It stretches. But eventually it hus tae snap. This is uncharted waters Jake, ye kin but try.
-   I've TRIED staying awake to see my family. Best I've managed is about 36 hours, that's with shit loads of coffee and I was pretty much a zombie then.
-   Drugs then. Ah've been up for 3 or 4 days on a speed binge.
-   Its money mate. I can't afford enough coke to last me an evening, speed, maybe two days.
-   Yir friendly wi' that Steve gadge arnae yous?

Jake mused about this. Yes, yes he was.

Chapter 40.

- 'Moan in.

Terry nodded a greeting and motioned with his head to Pete, Jim and Sarah. He looked bemused by Derek's presence, but offered him the same hospitality as the rest. Sarah felt impressed by how clean Terry's house was. She remembered it being a shit-hole when she had come back one night before. She looked at Terry, clean-shaven and thought he also looked like a shit-hole the last time she'd seen him. He must've cleaned up his act. Jim opted to blurt out the reason for their visit.

- Terry, I realise we haven't seen you in a while, but it's important it's…
- Jake, aye?
- Yeah, how did…?
- Ah've seen him. Time loop, trapped, same night, all mind o' memories that we brush off?
- Right. Yeah. So what do we need to do?

Terry sat down in his armchair.

- There's no much we kin do. The idea ah hud either didnae work or husnae work yet. Ah telt him if it didnae, tae come see me again. And he husn't.
- So we what? Wait here?
- Fuck off! We dinnae ken how long it will take if it works!

-   If what works?

Terry explained the plan he had given Jake in a clouded memory. He also explained how he wasn't sure if he would just sleep and the whole thing would never happen to any of them, or if Jake would suddenly hurtle though time to the present like a four-dimensional slingshot.

-   You all may as well leave. I'll let yis know if I get any new memories about whit's going on.

As they departed, Terry tensely bit his bottom lip. What if he was wrong?

Chapter 41.

Jake sat in his bedroom, which was by his own admission, a mess. He fancied it was a physical manifestation of his own chaotic mind. DVDs lined the walls, all purchased during a more successful time in his life. Broken cardboard boxes laid on the floor, half empty after he'd not fully unpacked after moving in six years prior. Discarded old sheets, duvets and pillows piled at the foot of his bed awaiting a trip to the bin that would likely never come. Despite the disorganised nature of the room, Jake was aware of where anything was at all times. As he gazed around the room, he considered starting the massive task of tidying and cleaning the room, before dismissing the notion because it was highly likely to return to the same state, should his experiment fail.

He pulled out his mobile phone and typed a text to his friend of sorts, Steve.

-    Can u cum 2 mine?

He closed the phone and contemplated playing video games until Steve arrived or contacted him back, but again chose not to, as they would be valuable in his plan on trying to stay awake for days. He lay back on his bed staring at the ceiling and imagined what it would be like to be out of this loop. As he warmed to his fantasy, his eyelids closed as he relaxed.

- Where to mate?
- Fuck! Shit! Fuck! Fuck! FUCKKKKKKK!!!

Jake yelled and punched the back of the seat in frustration back in the all too familiar taxi. The driver angrily ejected Jake from his cab and he stormed back inside his flat. Trying to calm himself, he re-sent the text message he had sent only minutes earlier in his world, yet in a different time-line to the one he was currently in.

He made his way to the kitchen to make himself a double-spooned coffee, resolute in the fact he would not let comfort impede his plans again. He waited impatiently for two hours that felt like five for an eventual knock on his door to see Steve smiling back at him.

- All right? Not going out tonight?
- Naw, got something I need to do. Need your help with it to be honest. C'mon in.

Steve entered the flat breezily, curls bouncing off his shoulders as he walked, making Jake seethe at how happy he appeared.

- So Jake, what can I help with?

Steve dropped onto the couch with a dull thud and looked at Jake with a broad smile.

- I need to stay awake for a week. I only have a hundred quid spare. Can you sort me a load of coke for that and let me get you for the rest later?
- You remember the rules man, no credit. Ever. I realise we're mates, but that can all change when money's involved. Besides man, Responsibility has to come forward here. Even if I could get you that amount of coke, you'd probs have a heart attack before the week is up.
- Speed then.
- Still talking a large quantity pal. And again, no credit. Hundred quid might see you through to Monday.
- So you're no use then. In this situation.

Steve took mild offence to the tone, but saw a desperation in Jake's eyes and thought of a solution.

- I might have the answer, but it isn't nice. Remember when M-Kat got banned? Well before that happened, I bought shit loads online. Literally sugar sized bags of the shit for fuck all. Now no-one wants it. It's a chav drug and I don't deal with chavs as you're aware. I'll do you that lot for a hundy. It's less than I paid at the time, but I've had it two years now and I'm not likely to shift it.
- I guess that will do. Cheers, I guess. Can I get a lift to yours, the cash machine and back?
- No worries. My advice, don't snort it or anything. Just mix some with water every now and again. It isn't pleasant,

but will keep you awake for at least eight hours at a time. Oh yeah, you might smell a bit like fish after a while, like your mam.

- Define 'not pleasant'.
- It's just shit stuff mate. It's plant food. It doesn't make you chattier or more energetic like speed and coke do. Plus drinking it can make you, not hallucinate, but look at things differently for a bit. Anyway, why do you need to stay awake for a week?
- Long story, experiment of sorts. I'll explain it to you if it all works at a later date.
- Fair enough. Let's get going then.

Jake and Steve made their way to Steve's modest car. It occurred to Jake that Steve was very careful about how he plied his trade and respected his caution. Too many idiots would show off any wealth around here in the same position. He estimated Steve easily pulled in over a grand a week just from his weekends, which involved hanging round the places he would go anyway and seeing everyone. Granted, it meant staying sober, but surely a small price to pay? Not for the first time, Jake considered his career choices had been poor ones.

As they continued their journey in relative silence, Jake gazed upon the areas of Grimsby he hadn't seen in so long, heading down the back streets towards Cleethorpes, on the way to Humberston where Steve lived. The areas at first got progressively worse as they headed through the East March, before improving as they drove past Sidney Park, where, as a child, he'd marvelled at the giant whale jawbone that had served as an entrance archway. He had fond memories walking through the park as an infant and toddler where a simple slide and a swing set had seemed like a day out.

A wave of nostalgia swept over Jake as he recalled his childhood years in the area he was travelling through. A cinema, long since closed around the corner from his former home with his parents taking him on a weekly basis to watch Disney films he slept through. One of his fondest memories was when they took him to see Clash of the Titans when his four-year-old mind got blown away by what unfurled on the screen in front of him. Excited and scared, he remembered leaving and being sat with a coke in the beer garden with his parents afterwards, pretending to fight 'snakeyhead'. It was the beginning of his lifelong love of film, not long afterwards seeing Empire Strikes Back at the same venue and again being overcome with awe.

He continued thinking about these times, being excited by the birth of his brother several years later, endless possibilities of mischief running through his young mind, being proud that he was the first person in the family to make his newborn brother laugh, teaching him swearwords that made him giggle until he was sick when Pete eventually repeated them. He missed his family more in this moment than he had in the entire fucked up situation he found himself in. This HAD to work. It had to.

Lost in thought, he barely noticed the rest of the journey. He collected the bags of shitty drugs and then dropped off home, thanking Steve and being genuinely grateful whilst doing so. In the kitchen he poured a small tumbler of water and mixed in a teaspoon of 'Meow Meow' into it, stirred and raised it to his lips. 'Here goes nothing', he thought to himself.

Chapter 42.

Natasha stared tearfully at the suitcase she'd recently unpacked for the fourth time that week. She thought after the memorial service for Jake, Pete would be more responsive and that they could finally move forward with their lives together. The opposite happened, he spent even more time with Jim and Sarah and became secretive. In her mind, at least before he talked about what went through his mind, but now he seemed secretive and unwilling to explain what was happening.

She briefly considered he'd been having a relationship with Sarah on the side and that he'd been using meeting with Jim as an alibi of sorts. Natasha realised this to be false as she'd seen him in the distance in town and followed, only to see them meet in Riverhead Coffee with some gangly guy she didn't recognise. She felt immense guilt for spying, but stood at her wits end. She held a deep love for Pete, but needed that to be returned with no need for spying or constant berating her partner into paying the attention she deserved.

Natasha's empty suitcase stared back at her accusingly. She imagined it scream at her to decide rather than flip-flopping on whether she should leave. She wanted to scream back at it that it wasn't that simple; it wasn't an easy decision to make; she didn't WANT to leave, but she was being pushed into a scenario where she had to; to recover, mourn the dead relationship and move on. She acknowledged it was just a suitcase and that shouting at it would be mental. Natahsa heard the key turn in the lock and she pushed the case back into the wardrobe in a hurry. She overheard Pete on his phone.

- Yeah, I know. I just dunno if I can keep waiting without trying to do something. Yeah. Yeah. I know. Fuck all we can do. See you later.
- Who's that?
- Jim.

Pete put his phone on the table and departed into the toilet. Natasha picked up the phone and looked at the call log. It was indeed, Jim. Guilt and shame washed over her for doubting his word. She placed the phone back down and sat on the couch, still in turmoil over what to do. Pete emerged from the bathroom and wrapped his arms around her from behind the couch. He kissed her tenderly on the forehead and squeezed tighter with his arms, which offered a slight amount of comfort.

- Things will be better soon.

His grip tightened and elicited fresh, silent tears from her. She wanted his words to be true. Natasha reciprocated the tight hug by raising her hand above her head to bring his closer to hers.

She would give it a little more time.

Chapter 43.

Jake tried in vain to concentrate on playing video games after ingesting the M-Kat concoction. He seemed warm unnaturally and the room throbbed around him. The grinning face of the Joker on a painting on his wall seemed to be malevolently grinning directly at him and he considered it sentient. The sensations he experienced weren't pleasant, and he questioned why anyone would take this shit recreationally. Then he remembered Steve's words about only chavs taking it and realised that it only an idiot chav, or himself, would. At least with other similar drugs, they offered a sense of invincibility and that your words were powerful tools, to be shared with the world for their benefit. Now he felt powerless and a little scared.

He made his way shakily downstairs to have a glass of water. He lamented his decision to undertake this test and wondered if it was worth it. Even in his warped logical state, he could see that a week of unpleasantness would far outweigh a lifetime trapped in the same evening repeatedly. After several glasses of water, he regained a little more control of his faculties and again tried playing video games in his room. This time he could do it with aplomb and was proud to complete Dark Souls. Even happier still when he looked at his clock and realised that 30 hours passed without even a whiff of sleep threatening to overcome him. He prepared another cocktail of plant food dilute and optimism buoyed him on.

Jake realised that soon it would be time to go to his parents for the Sunday dinner he never got to see. He rang Pete to let him know he wasn't going. A brief reunion with his family would make him comfortable, and possibly tired. He couldn't risk it as much as he wanted to. He lied to Pete and told him he was ill, which Pete assumed to be a hangover, but seemed strangely relieved to hear from him for reasons he wasn't quite sure of. Jake went back to his room and started Borderlands to see him through to Monday. In the morning, he dutifully called his work to inform them he wouldn't be in, still remembering the Sword of Damocles hanging over his head regarding employment and figured that he should try to keep some income flowing for at least a little while.

- Good morning, Jobcentre plus, Blaire speaking, how can I help?

Jake cursed. He hated Blaire with a passion. He'd frequently described her as a 'grade A cunt' to anyone that would listen.

- Err Yeah, It's Jake, I won't be in today. Or for a while actually. I feel awful.

Blaire audibly sighed. Jake thought she was an unprofessional bitch.

- Ok. I need to go through a checklist of questions. What is the nature of your condition?
- I want to die. I've had enough. I can't take anymore.

Jake was surprised by his own candour. Usually he would be vague. Blaire sighed again. This time Jake's anger refused to let that slide.

- What are you sighing for? Pretty sure there's some kind of process when people call in saying things like this. It's hardly professional is it?
- I didn't sigh.
- Well add 'hallucinating' to the list as well then. For fucks sake.
- If you carry on swearing, I'm ending the call.
- I didn't swear. My auditory hallucinations must be contagious. Let's crack on with this shall we?

Jake took comfort because he'd taken control of the conversation. In his mind he knew there were no real downsides to it anyway, since his job was effectively being ended by this period of sickness and if the worst came to the worst, he could simply go to sleep and reset it. With this in mind he became quite buoyant.

- Do you have a doctor's note?
- No I don't. It is a quarter past eight on a Monday morning.
- Will you be visiting the doctors?

- Yes, I'll bring it in.
- Can you do alternative duties?
- What magical alternative duties do you suggest will alleviate this bout of severe ennui?
- Well, like filing, posting letters and such.
- Such a tempting offer. Pass.
- So you're refusing?
- I'm saying I'm not well enough. Exactly which part of 'I want to die' was vague to you?
- Well sometimes being active can help with...
- Stuffing letters in envelopes will not change this! You're not a doctor, stop pretending you have any level of expertise on these matters and just fill in your dumb form and let me go in peace!

Jake heard another intake of breath on the phone, this time steeling Blaire for the question he knew was due to follow. He relished making her uncomfortable, in the same way she'd done to him for the many years he'd worked there.

- Will you be back at work this afternoon if your condition improves?
- That you even asked that shows a staggering level of ignorance. And that you have paid no attention to what I'm saying.
- You do realise that I will report your attitude don't you?

- Go ahead. And I'll report the fact that you didn't go through the mandatory suicide checklist we are all supposed to do. The calls are recorded don't forget. Your sighing and lack of sensitivity towards a vulnerable member of staff will be exposed. I wonder exactly who would be hauled over the coals the most? Me, someone in a fragile state of mind, or you, someone who has to constantly hammer home the point that we are all supposed to show empathy on the phones. Do it. I'll have a lot to say in that meeting. And who knows? If I top myself, maybe my family can sue.
- I'll just put 'no' for that one shall I?
- Yes, you shall. We done?
- You want me to go through the suicide checklist?
- Sarcasm now is it? You're making this too easy. Don't bother, I know it off by heart.
- Don't forget, you need to bring the note in today and ring every day to keep us informed.
- Yeah, I won't be doing that. The note will cover me. Bye

Jake clicked off his mobile grinning at the fact he'd annoyed Blaire. Small victories were worth savouring he considered. He then realised he would have to actually leave his flat to get the doctors' note and the small victory was deflated. Although he was wide awake, his energy levels were low, partially through lack of sleep, but also because he hadn't eaten since

Friday. He drank another glass of the vile mixture and proceeded to his doctor's surgery.

Jake panicked as he arrived, assuming he'd slept through the bus journey, that he was there at the surgery entrance meant that he hadn't fallen asleep, to his relief, but he was concerned by the fact he didn't have a single memory or acknowledgement of the journey. He checked the time. 10:39 am. He entered the surgery.

Jake emerged from the surgery, again with no memory of being inside. He again checked the time 12:11pm. What happened? In his pocket he found a prescription for 20mg capsules of Citalopram and a leaflet for Open Minds. He considered he may have oversold his mental state a little to be sent to the mental health team. He started back towards the bus stop to his flat.

Another loss of time seemed to occur as Jake shook back into focus and found he'd walked almost the entire journey. These lapses concerned him and he vowed not to leave his home again until after this ordeal had finished. But first, he needed to drop off the fit note to the DWP office. He stopped at a café to drink and eat, to hopefully stop the blank spots from happening.

It didn't work. He suddenly found himself stood in the car park of the ugly building he hated so much, the one he'd previously considered throwing himself off the top of. He punched in his security code and entered the building.

Another skip, he was walking towards home, not knowing if he'd accomplished his goals. He checked his pocket for the fit note and it had gone. He checked his phone. 13:49. Time checked out. He'd three text messages from concerned colleagues asking if he was ok. 'U looked lyk a zombie!' one joked. So he'd been inside. The worst was over and he needed to lock himself away from the outside world that was scaring him so much, one he could remember less and less interacting with.

Four days to go, he mused, before blacking out again and coming to in his bedroom in front of his PlayStation. This time, Mass Effect was on the screen. He was halfway through.

Chapter 44.

Pete lay awake in bed late in the evening whilst Natasha slept next to him. He thought about his life and what it had become. Guilt swept over him on the way he'd reacted with Derek and despite wanting desperately to apologise for it and explain it to be a culmination of the frustration of the past year, he couldn't find the right time or the right words. He vowed to at least make it up to him in some small way, perhaps by offering the friendship he clearly craved.

He gazed across at the sleeping figure of Natasha. Her brow furrowed in fitful sleep, he still found her as beautiful as the day he met her. He realised he'd been neglecting her for quite some time, locked in his inability to get over his brother's disappearance. Pete stroked hair from her face and she murmured in slight agitation. He sensed her growing distant and spotted her suitcase had moved several times; he worried that he was losing her. He wanted to wake her up and hold her; tell her everything would be all right. He grew determined to make more of an effort since he now was certain there was nothing possible to find Jake except wait. Any conversations with Scotch Terry had now dried up as he'd moved away, pursuing physics qualifications since his passion had been re-ignited. The change in Terry had been startling and whilst sad to see him go, he was pleased that some good came out of this for someone.

His thoughts returned to Natasha and how he would begin repairing the damage he'd caused. He loved her intensely and realised how much she'd put up with from him. He cried silently faced with the prospect of losing her, cradling her head with his hand whilst he did so. Natasha awoke, not noticing the tears.

- What's up?
- Nothing. Just thinking.
- About Jake?
- No. About you. I'm... I'm sorry I've not been there.
- What? What brought this on?
- I realise I've been shitty. That changes now. No matter what happens. I still need you in my life. We go out for dinner tomorrow. Spend some time together, spend a lot of time together. Sound good?

Natasha responded with a hug. As she did so, she felt the wetness of his cheeks on her bare shoulder, whilst elicited tears of her own. She didn't know if the change of heart was permanent, but yeah. Dinner sounded good.

Chapter 45.

Jake stood motionless aside from a slight sway in front of his living room window. The curtains drawn, but Jake still appeared to be watching the outside. His mouth hung open with a long string of drool slowly making its way down his clothing. His jeans still damp with urine from a few hours earlier, but he'd not noticed this as his mind seemed to be absent.

Suddenly, his sway became a tilt, and he crashed down to the floor with a thud. Jake swore, but was back in control and scrabbled for his phone. Thursday dinnertime. He'd lost another ten or so hours. Jake had long abandoned the idea of trying to play games since his consciousness missed most of the game, anyway. He viewed his pissy jeans in distaste, so ran a bath and got a change of clothes, bundling the soiled clothing in the washing machine. He feared he may die, or be killed by someone unidentified that he was becoming increasingly afraid of. The last thing he wanted if he was to die, was to be found in the state he was in.

Another couple of hours passed. Jake's mind seemed to crash back into his body with a jolt and he realised he lay in a tepid bath. He got out and dried himself off and caught his reflection in the mirror. He looked like shit, whether it be from almost a week's M-Kat fuelled sleep-depravation, or that he considered he generally looked like a sack of shit, it made him angry.

- Fucking shit fat cunt useless bastard ugly piece of fucking shit! Cunt! Cunt! Fucking worthless CUUUUUUUNNNTTTT!

Jake bellowed at his reflection as it crumbled into multiple pieces as he slammed his fist repeatedly into the mirror. Shards of glass flew all over the bathroom and the walls became coated with blood spatter from his cut-up knuckles. He slumped naked against the bath sobbing. Was it worth it? Am I worth it? The two phrases echoed through his mind as he waited for another blackout to come.

Mercifully, it came, when sentient again, he still sat in the same spot. Six hours had passed. He knew this from the phone in front of him and the fact that in his mind's absence, he'd carved a five-bar gate into his left arm. It was now early Friday morning. A few more hours. He dressed himself and winced as he stepped on shards of broken mirror. One more glass of this shit stuff he thought. Best make it a big one.

Again, his mind was absent for several hours, coming back to in a body that had paced around aimlessly. His calves and ankles cramped from however long he had been doing this. Again he checked his phone. Midday Friday. It was over. He could sleep. He staggered to his bedroom and collapsed on the bed and waited for genuine sleep to pass over him for the first time in a year. Frustratingly, sleep would not come. He guessed he needed to flush out any of the vile drug from his system, so wearily trudged to his kitchen and drank as much water as he was able, after which, he spent a long time urinating before flopping down in an exhausted heap on his bed.

Jake lay for a while imagining the reunion between him, his family and friends. He didn't know if this would work, but their images comforted him. He closed his eyes.

And then he was gone.

Chapter 46.

It was morning. Cold February sun shone through the crack in the curtains. Normally Jake hated this, but he hadn't seen it in so long, it seemed welcoming. He got out of bed and looked out of the window. It was definitely daytime. He wasn't in a taxi. He beamed and went to shower, to prepare for the long overdue chance to visit his parents, brother and friends to have a different conversation.

After showering, he walked through the living room with a large mug of tea, feeling positive. As he was about to sit, he heard a knock at the door. Excitedly, he put down his mug and waddled to the door as fast as he could. His good mood was short lived as he opened the door to spot *her.* She was accompanied by the other *her.*

- Clarice? Katie? What in the fuck do you two want?
- Aww Jake. You still mad at us?
- Of course I'm still mad at you. You're a cunt and she's a psychopath. I want nothing to do with you.
- Yet you will still let us in any way.

Clarice smiled and cocked her head as she waltzed past Jake into his flat. Katie walked past too, a flat smile, never changing, that seemed fixed to her lips. Her eyes were wide as she held Jake's gaze walking past him after Clarice. Jake checked his wallet was in his back pocket and secured his mobile in the front. As he followed them through, he scanned the room for small, easy to steal items. Happy he'd left none around he sat down.

- I repeat my question; What the FUCK do you want?
- To say sorry, silly. Why else would we be here?
- I honestly couldn't begin to fathom what goes on in either of your fucked-up brains. Here's a guess, you want to prop up your own ego, and she wants to nick something?
- Ha-ha. You always were funny Jake. We want to try again.

Clarice was doing all the talking, but Katie nodded in affirmation, the smile not flinching for a second. Jake shuddered. His mind raced for ways to get rid of these women. Seeing them was enough to ruin his mood, let alone having them in proximity talking about a reconciliation. Clarice walked over and sat closer to him, stroking his arm with one hand and edging the other round his shoulders. Katie's eyes widened.

- We were young. Everyone makes mistakes. You made enough of them too, remember? But we both talked and felt bad about how things turned out and want to get back together.
- There are two of you! For fucks sake, this is stupid. I want you to leave.
- Exactly. Two of us. That's what you've always wanted deep down. So will you go out with us?

- I'll pass.
- Great! We will be so happy the three of us!

Clarice stood up grabbing hold of Jake's hand and kissing it lightly. Katie clapped her hands together in silence and crossed the room to hug him. The smile seemed almost painted on her face, never faltering, never broadening. Jake clambered away tugging his hand from Clarice's surprisingly strong grasp.

- I said no! You really are a pair of mental bitches!
- Yeah... but you meant yes! So it's all good!

Jake got scared. His impotence grew in the face of her insistence and he questioned if he'd actually responded in the negative at all, or just agreed and internalised a refusal. Suddenly, he found himself in his room with the both of them, Katie slowly removing her trousers showing the arse that once seemed so perfect, it made him forgive her in the past. Clarice straddled him, topless, her breasts looking better than they ever did in his memory. How did he get here? He asked himself and then wondered if the week on M-Kat was still blacking things out now it was all over. Clarice bit on her bottom lip as she reached behind her, massaging Jake's crotch until he had the most unwelcome erection he'd ever possessed. He didn't want this.

- I don't want this. Get off me
- Yes you do, I can tell.

Clarice squeezed at his hard-on through his jeans as she spoke, Katie reached over and did the same, the smile parting to allow a pleased gasp to pass her lips. She reached over Clarice's toned thigh, stroking it lightly, causing Clarice to softly moan in appreciation. Jake watched her fingers work their way under the waistband of Clarice's underwear, creating a fresh wave of louder moans. Jake looked away.

- I don't want this. Please. Just go.
- Watch.

Clarice roughly grabbed Jake's chin as Katie edged closer to her, removing her bra as she did so. She held his cheeks in place as she turned to kiss her, both women's hands busy over each other's bodies. Clarice shuffled herself backwards, grinding herself against Jake's cock, tongue in Katie's mouth, both gazing at Jake as if it were a performance, or a porno. Jake shifted uncomfortably and shouted.

- Stop!
- You don't want us to stop. Remember how much you wanted a three-way? Well here it is, with the two people you know you still love.
- I don't fucking love either of you. I despise both of you. Get the fuck off me now!

As Jake bucked, Clarice's arms pinned his down with surprising speed and forced as she shifted her weight forwards onto his chest while Katie held down his legs and unbuckled his fly, tugging furiously at the belt to loosen the cock he currently wished he didn't have. She succeeded and continued to smile before opening her mouth and going down to the hilt.

- You say you don't want it, but you're harder than you've ever been in your life. And it's for both of us. Stop trying to fight it and kiss me.

Jake thrashed as hard as he could, pushing Katie aside with his leg, causing her eyes to flash with anger, but the smile remained, tight lipped as ever as she started towards him again. He turned back to focus his energies on Clarice who giggled before bring her head down full force onto the bridge of Jake's nose. Jake barely had time to shake off the stars before she punched him repeatedly, each blow making him hear a loud crunch in his head. He watched Katie, laid next to him, the smile now gone, replaced by a smooth patch of skin where her mouth should be. She stared at him whilst Clarice rained down blows and he realised she was masturbating to the scenario. His erection at least, had disappeared.

Clarice screamed at him.

- You fucking useless bastard; we came to offer you what you wanted! You can't be happy can you? You're never fucking happy unless you're making others miserable are you?

She thrust her face close to his and hissed. Her skin appeared grey as did Katie's and there was no longer sunlight poking in through the curtains. As Jake coughed and spat to clear his face of blood as best he could without the use of his arms, he noticed that both women's eyes were red and their teeth were becoming sharper. Clarice poked his skull with her index finger, which seemed elongated and more painful than the head-butt or any of the punches she threw.

-    We live here now. We will always live here. Cunt.

Jake was relieved when blackness washed over him.

Chapter 47.

Jake awoke with a start in the same clothes he wore on the night out. He'd similar dreams in the past, trapped in an unwanted relationship with Clarice or Katie, but things never escalated or got as horrific as this particular dream. As the thankful realisation it was merely his subconscious at work took hold, he realised several key points. He'd been asleep, a sensation foreign to him after the last year. He wasn't in the taxi, something surprisingly disorienting to him, even more so was that he appeared to be in his room, but on the floor in an empty version of it save for a few cardboard boxes.

Jake clambered to his feet, staggering as he stood and took stock of his surroundings. Familiar, yet alien to him at the same time he slowly made his way through the flat, noting that the other room now had a bed in it, with the snoring figure of an old man visible through the partially opened door. He panicked, knowing he was trespassing in his own home, reasoning if time passed, it was likely to have been let to another person in his absence. If this was the case where was all of his stuff? Jake shook his head, his primary goal now to leave quickly and try to figure out what happened later. He crept towards the front door and was relieved to spot keys in the lock. As silently as possible, he turned them and took them out. He locked the door behind him after his exit and posting the keys back through the letter-box. It wouldn't be right to leave an old man in an unlocked flat asleep in this neighbourhood, he thought, even if he was in his home.

He shakily made his way down the street heading towards central Grimsby town centre. He checked his mobile and initially thought no time had passed looking at the date. Only upon a double take did he notice it was exactly a year later. He tried to call Pete, but there was no service. It figured as in this new 'time' he wouldn't have paid his bill. His next course of action was to check if he had money left in his bank account, then get to a place that allowed free Wi-Fi to orient himself whilst contacting his loved ones. He checked his wallet for his cash card. Shit! It had expired. Now he'd the added complication of going in the bank too. He quickened his pace, squinting against the bright sunshine that promised a temperature far higher than the cold February air delivered.

After a ten minute walk, leaving Jake exhausted, he walked past the Barge towards the bus station when he heard a semi-familiar voice shout.

-    Jake! JAAAAKKKEE! You're back!

Jake turned to spot a figure he didn't initially recognise running towards him with a broad smile. He was dressed differently, not smarter, but with jeans, t-shirt and jacket and more length to his hair, the figure he eventually recognised as Derek looked less severe, non-descript almost, but certainly friendly. Despite himself, Jake felt happy to see him. In his enthusiasm to cross the distance between them, Derek glanced his shoulder against a post, spinning him, causing his shin to collide with a sickening crack against a nearby bench. This resulted in a stumbling backwards fall, momentum carrying his head onto the concrete with a thud. Wincing in empathy, Jake started over towards him and was relieved that Derek was OK, still smiling, rubbing the back of his head and limping quickly over.

- Jesus! Scr... Derek... are you OK?
- Never mind that! S'alright! You're back!

Derek grabbed him and threw his arms around him in a crushing hug that Jake considered a little unwelcome at first, but glad he'd seen a somewhat familiar face in this confusing time. He broke away from the hug that carried on a little too long for his tastes.

- Seriously, are you all right, your head hit the ground with a bang.
- I've had worse. You're back!
- This has been established.
- I know! But you're back!

Jake suspected Derek suffered a minor concussion.

- Yep. I'm back. And kind of lost at the minute. Can't ring anyone, need to go to the bank. Everything is different. I think I'm homeless. I need to ring Pete and my family.

- I'll ring him!

Derek pulled out his phone and selected Pete's number and dialled. Jake was surprised that he'd got it. Derek looked forlorn as he stared at his phone.

- I've run out of credit. Sorry Jake.
- Doesn't matter. I'll go to the bank and get some money. I'll buy you a coffee at Riverhead.
- Ok! Sorry about that.
- It's fine. Appreciate the offer.

Jake and Derek walked to the bank in silence. Jake discovered that withdrawing his money wasn't the aggravation he'd expected. His account hadn't closed, and with his birth certificate and an old card, it enabled him to take out some money and check his balance, which was shockingly over £13,000. He looked at the deposits and noticed monthly payments from his employer and wondered why they'd continued. Jake observed a reduction in the amount and figured they probably didn't have an exact process for people off sick who'd gone missing. He couldn't complain at the result, but cursed himself for not paying his bills by direct debit. He would still have a home and a phone if that had been the case. His mistrust of that system hoisted him by his own petard.

They made their way down the street to Jake's favourite coffee shop and he connected to the Wi-Fi and dialled his brother's number on WhatsApp. Aggravated that there was no response, he sipped his coffee contemplating the next move when his mobile rang to life. Pete. He answered excitedly.

- Pe…
- Who the fuck is this?
- It's me Pete. I'm back
- Fuck off whoever it is. This isn't funny.
- Don't hang up! It's really me! I'm with Derek, who I believe you are now acquainted with?
- Yeah, Pete it's me! He is really here!
- Fuck! Serious?! Where are you?
- At Riverhead. Shit is weird. I'm kind of frayed, not knowing what to do. How come you're able to ring my phone?
- Oh yeah… they kept the line open for incoming calls cos you went missing. I'll explain that later. Details. I'm leaving work. I'll be with you in a bit! Fuck! I'm so glad to speak to you!.

Jake realised his brother's voice cracked a little and felt emotional himself. He couldn't imagine how hard this affected Pete or his family. Guilt washed over him for what he perceived as wallowing in how it'd been for him all of this time. He also experienced shame for considering ending it all and how others would have seen it as a betrayal. Derek seemed to notice and placed a reassuring hand on his shoulder.

-   Take it easy man. One thing at a time.

As the two, now seemingly firm friends talked awaiting the arrival of Pete, Jake had a fair few gaps filled in by Derek. He learned of Scotch Terry's 'epiphany' as the group all kept in touch, reminding each other of the 'memories' that may or may not have happened in each respective version of events. Jake was pleased that Terry now had a renewed focus in life. He hoped they would catch up in the future, crediting him for the experiment that appeared to have worked.

Derek also explained how he, Sarah, Jim and Pete all became friends during this time. They spent a lot of time together, partially forced by the knowledge that only they shared and frequent, desperate brain-storming sessions of potential solutions to the problem, none of which made any sense to Derek, or to each other it seemed. So they continued doing the only thing possible and waited. Finally Pete arrived, rushing up the stairs and stopping dead upon seeing his brother for the first time in a year. With glassy eyes he crossed the room and threw his arms around Jake, who reciprocated, also welling up as he did so. When they finally let each other go, Pete turned to Derek.

-   Thanks man. For letting me know first.
-   You needed to know first. Jake tried but his phone was cut off.

Jake wanted to speak, but was unable as he feared the second he uttered a sound he would burst into tears. As he tried to compose himself, Pete helped him by suggesting one of the many things he wanted to do.

-   We'll have to get you round mum and dad's pretty sharpish. Do you want to meet up with everyone later?

Jake nodded, glad of the opportunity to continue not speaking.

-   Cool. Derek, while we are back home, can you get in touch with Jim and Sarah? Let them know and get them to round others up?
-   Yeah, no worries.
-   Say 8 o'clock? Matrix sound good?

Jake grew alarmed by the prospect. It was the last place he wanted to go right now. Although, logistically, it made sense. Finally able to speak, he responded, careful to not sound unenthusiastic.

-   Yeah. Matrix sounds good.

Chapter 48.

Jake sat emotionally exhausted. His reunion with his parents had been several hours of tears and hugs that never seemed to end. But he wouldn't have changed it for the world. His parents had been quick to 'do up' the spare room, so he'd somewhere to stay as he was now homeless. Also, the prospect of having proper cooked meals enticed him.

Through the conversations, Jake learned he still possessed a job at the DWP. They'd continued to pay sick pay during his absence, full pay for six months, half pay for the rest. Despite what he'd been through, the prospect of ever going back there galled him, so he vowed to go to the doctors again to get signed off and await the inevitable pay out that would result from his termination. After being trapped in the same evening, he'd grown determined to get as much pleasure as possible out of life. Money would eventually become a concern, but that was nothing compared to the abject misery being there caused him. Even with a year gone by without the job, his chest tightened with the prospect of one more day.

Connected to Wi-Fi again, his phone buzzed almost constantly as word spread of his return and people posted variations of welcome back onto his Facebook wall. At first he checked and responded to each one, then got irritated by it, seeing messages from people who never bothered with him when he was actually around, but apparently 'missed him dearly'. His cynicism had returned, and he tried to squash it down. He didn't want to think like that anymore.

As he relaxed on the sofa in his parental home, his mother fussing over bedding for the spare room and his father slowly dozing off after the afternoon's excitement, he spotted figures in the conservatory in the gloom of early evening. As he squinted to better see who they were, the glowing red eyes appeared, and he noticed Clarice and Katie staring malevolently back at him, as they did at the end of the dream, half naked with their skin now seeming a waxy grey. Clarice pointed with her long fingers and grinned, revealing way too many teeth, pointed and sharp. Katie's mouthless visage stared wider, and she seemed to emit a high pitched squeal. He closed his eyes and re-opened them. They'd gone. Had he got some sort of psychosis? Or was this an after-effect of a week on M-Kat?

Jake and Pete left their parents' house for central town to meet the rest of their friends, placating their put-out parents as they did so. They walked, since Pete planned on having a celebratory drink. As they walked past the Barge, Pete cursed and stabbed his phone to call Natasha and let her know what had happened. Whilst his brother apologised/ explained to his girlfriend for his lapse in memory, a scruffy figure approached him. Unkempt, greasy ginger hair clung to his forehead, Jake recognised him as the 'cheeky Hull guy', who'd harangued everyone in the area for money for several years now.

- Ay oop mert! Y'got 86p fer a cheeky 'Ull lad?
- Welcome back to GY...
- Eh?
- No I don't, fuck off.
- Come on mert! Ah need ter get back ter 'Ull!
- Then stop coming to fucking Grimsby then! You've been doing this for fucking years now! If you don't have the bus fare to get home, don't go on a journey! Unless of course... it isn't for the bus... and you're just begging for cash for smack or special brew or whatever it is that makes you consider it acceptable to ask for a very specific amount of cash, possibly one that could be easily rounded up to a quid? Fuck off you fucking bag-head!
- Yer fooking arrogant mert! Ah need ter ger 'ome. Ah'm not on fooking smack or ert! Ah'll fooking smack yer!

Pete noticed the commotion as he ended the call with Natasha. She'd been miffed he hadn't contacted her, but relieved it was all finally over and would meet them later. Pete made his way over as Jake snarled and took a step towards the irritating guy, who then yelped and full on sprinted in the other direction, causing both to erupt into fits of giggles. 'Jake is back', Pete happily mused.

As they entered Matrix a few minutes later, it became clear Derek had gone above and beyond in contacting people. The downstairs area was full of people who all cheered loudly as they entered the room. Pete smiled at Jake, who was touched by how many people showed up for him, despite his earlier misgivings about people who hadn't bothered with him for years. This was real, not an attention seeking slab of text on social media. He wouldn't forget it.

Jake was taken aback by the change in the room. It had been re-furbished and reflected more what the place was about. Guitars lined the walls of the area leading to the toilets, one side of the wall covered with comic book scenes, another with posters and artworks from various cult films and TV shows. It showed that the venue was now a rock pub run by comic geeks and film nerds. Jake approved.

As he caught up with people, careful to not drink, Jake slowly relaxed. The idea of going to the place he'd spent the last year had been off-putting, but the warmth he felt from the genuine smiles and well wishes buoyed his spirits and gave him a sense of belonging. Jim and Derek barely left his side all evening, ushering him back and forth between people they'd contacted. Jake wanted to ask where Sarah was, but didn't want it to seem like he suggested they hadn't done enough.

His questions got answered moments later when he watched her walk in. He realised why she was late. At that moment she looked the most beautiful he'd ever seen her. She'd obviously spent a long time getting ready. His mind flooded back to the time they spent together, ones which she wouldn't be able to fully remember and suffered a pang of loss. As life carried on, he was certain being with her was all he wanted and hoped that by some miracle she wanted the same. She hadn't seen him yet. He headed outside for a calming cigarette beforehand and walked past her whilst she had her back to him waiting to be served.

He smoked outside and pondered his next move whilst smoking. Thankfully, due to the cold, he'd no distractions from other people as he smoked.

- I can't let you stand out here alone can I?

Sarah beamed with tears in her eyes. Jake lost count of the amount of times he'd been the same that day and didn't want to ruin his 'manly' aura, so tried to make light of the situation.

- I've been away for a year. You could have made an effort to get dressed up all nice for me when I got back.

Sarah laughed as the tears brimmed over falling down her cheek and squeezed him hard. He folded his arms around her too and didn't want to let go. As they rested their heads on each other's shoulders, Jim walked out of the door, noting the scenario, smiled and walked back inside.

Sarah's hands moved up and down his body, caressing him as they embraced. He took the cue and did the same, both pulling their heads apart and gazing into the others' eyes before their mouths forcibly collided into a kiss, a year in waiting for Sarah, less so for Jake. They continued probing their mouths with their tongues like teenagers drunk on cider. Jake was overjoyed because for once, he seemed have something go right for him. The sharp intake of breath from Sarah's nostrils made the blood rush to his cock. Sarah felt this against her thigh and giggled. She contemplated doing something she never did and initiating sex outside the comforts of her own home when Jake crumpled to the floor clutching his head.

Jake never suffered a pain so intense in his life. A high pitched squeal became a full on throbbing shriek, seemingly emanating from inside his head. Sarah looked on aghast as he writhed and stopped thrashing. Slowly opening his eyes at something behind her, and his eyes widening with terror. She looked over her shoulder and noted nothing was there.

Nothing wasn't what Jake had seen. He'd eyed Katie, perched on a barbed wire fence partition between the Matrix beer garden and the Witherspoon's next door. Her bony, claw like hand planted in between her legs rubbing vigorously as her narrowed red eyes stared back at him with hate. Clarice laid back on a nearby bench, laughing uncontrollably, slapping the table with her hand. She sat upright with a start and glared menacingly at Jake.

-   Oh no. Not on our watch. Little miss slutty-tits will have to go elsewhere. You belong to us. Cunt.

The figures seemed to dissipate as Jake gripped onto Sarah tightly as she cradled and stroked his head. The pain subsided, and he feared psychosis had taken a hold on him. As he started towards Sarah to kiss her, to apologise; a faint squeal vibrated through his skull, which dissolved as he pulled away.

-   I'm… I'm sorry. I don't… I'm not… right yet. I had to take a lot of…
-   Don't worry. We've got plenty of time. I dunno how hard this has been on you, or how it has affected you. Go home. Rest. There is a tomorrow now.

Sarah smiled and hugged him again. He hoped she was right. Now he'd acknowledged his feelings for her, he wasn't sure if it would be possible to go back. He loved her, although he wouldn't say it out loud just yet, he also needed her, he became convinced his future happiness depended on it. He braved the squeal for a fairly quick kiss as he staggered to his feet.

-   Ok. That's probably it. Brain got fried. I need to sleep properly. Haven't done it in a year. Look, I'm groggy, can you let everyone know I've left?
-   Of course I can. Can we catch each other tomorrow?

- I don't reckon I want anything more than that.

Sarah smiled and kissed Jake's cheek, running her hand down his arm and slowly letting go of his hand as she walked away. He walked backwards for a few steps smiling as he held her gaze until she went back inside. Turning, he walked towards the taxi rank at the train station around the corner, getting in the first cab in the queue.

As he sat in the front of the taxi, he immediately recognised it as the one he'd begun every evening in for the past year. Panic crept in and faded as he realised the car had aged, no longer the plushest of interiors, yet still clean. The driver grinned in recognition.

- All right mate? Been a long time. Where to?
- It has. Wybers please, I'll direct you from there.

The stereo crackled into life with a familiar piano intro he remembered from his youth. From the front seat he glanced at the driver's I.D.; Garry Fiacre. In all the time he'd been trapped, it never occurred to him to ask his name. Was that ignorant? Probably not. To Garry, it was only one evening, or possible others when he'd been in the car in the past.

You know I'm a dreamer, but my heart's of gold

The song began. Another classic. Jake perceived a strange comfort in this car. Possibly because of the shared taste in music. He smiled and pointed at the stereo, reciprocated by Garry.

I had to run away high, so I wouldn't come home low

Sarah dominated his mind. He hoped the Clarice and Katie hallucinations were a temporary thing. Jake likened himself to the end of the Shawshank Redemption; crawling through a tunnel of shit to come up smelling of roses at the other end. Life had potential again

Just when things went right, It doesn't mean they were always wrong

He struggled to figure out how the rest of everyone 'remembered' all the different times. Also, how would he going to explain his absence to people? He'd tried explaining it to his parents, but they assumed he'd been drugged, which wasn't too far from the truth, but not the explanation. Amnesia? Kidnapping? The truth was clearly too unbelievable. At least Sarah had the truth. That was important to him.

Take me to your heart, Feel me in your bones. Just one more night and I'm coming off this long and winding road.

Play it by ear. Jake considered himself better at off-the-cuff responses than carefully planned out ones. Or just stick to the truth and let others make their own version up. His mind raced.

I'm on my way.

- You look knackered mate.
- Yeah. It's been a long... night.
- I can imagine. Get some rest. You'll need it.

The fuck does he mean by that? Maybe nothing. I probably misheard him. Jake screwed his face and entertained the notion he'd developed PTSD or something like that.

I'm on my wa-a-a-yyyy

He observed the familiar roads of the estate where he spent his formative years. He gave Garry further instructions and looked forward to a decent night's sleep. The other stuff was bound to sort itself out and fade. Go forward. Forget the night out. Time to do something else.

Home sweet home.

Epilogue.

The heat hit Jake as if opening an oven door mid-cook. Bright sunlight seared his retinas as he scrabbled into the pockets of his long leather coat for his sunglasses. Placing them on, he tried to take stock of his surroundings, his eyes seeing small blue sparks momentarily.

He was surrounded by tall buildings, skyscrapers and Asian writing on gaudy billboards everywhere. Thousands of Asian people surrounded him and they appeared to be speeding up from an almost standstill. Jake continued to gaze up at the unfamiliar buildings, the height of them making him dizzy looking up to. He took off his coat; he was already covered in sweat. His coat appeared sticky as if something had been spilt on it, yet he couldn't remember what. How the hell did I get here?

He walked further down the road and turned into a small alleyway, partially to get some shade and also to avoid the throngs of face-mask wearing people propelling him forwards. Jake looked out from the alleyway and saw road signs in both English and Asian.

He continued down the alleyway and was surprised it led to what appeared to be a large indoor market. As he carried on, bewildered by his surroundings, he was glad to feel a blast of cool air coming from an old air conditioning vent on the ceiling. As he stopped, a man in a shirt and tie with a white surgical mask covering his face accidentally collided with him.

- Sumimasen

Jake didn't understand what the man had said, but took it as an apology and nodded in response. Open mouthed he continued to gawp at the shops and people. He was scared, disoriented and also enticed. Jake closed his mouth and continued to stand in the same area, enjoying the cooling sensation his sweat had on his over-heating body thanks to the cold air. He spoke to no-one in particular.

- How the fuck did I get to China?

Acknowledgments.

So many people to thank for helping me to write this book. It's my first attempt, and I was unsure of myself for many years before finally sitting down and trying. So firstly, thanks to Dave H who listened to my original idea and encouraged me to write it, saying it was cool and going as far as to lending me a laptop since mine was slow as shit with sticky keys. Thanks to Holly, Dave P and Hal who read through during the entire process giving me feedback and compliments that spurred me on even when my terminal laziness didn't want me to. Thanks as well to Gilly for helping keep me sane over the past few months.

Also, thanks to my family and friends for putting up with me and also for helping me through the worst of times. This book is dedicated to all of you.

Thanks as well to Clare W. Just because I said I would ☺

Also big thanks to Riverhead Coffee for keeping me plied with coffee whilst I wrote this, sat there in a coffee shop with a laptop like a fucking cliché—you never once made me feel a dick for it. Also, thanks to The Barge, The Matrix, Lloyds Arms and Gulliver's for all the nights out, some good, some bad. There is very little personality left in pubs and clubs in the UK now and all of those have kept individuality against the rolling tide of shitty chain pubs.

And a final cliché; thank you for reading this. I hope you enjoyed it. I also hope you will enjoy the sequels. Things will get bat-shit crazy

Jake will return in 'Backbones', part 2 of the triloGY.

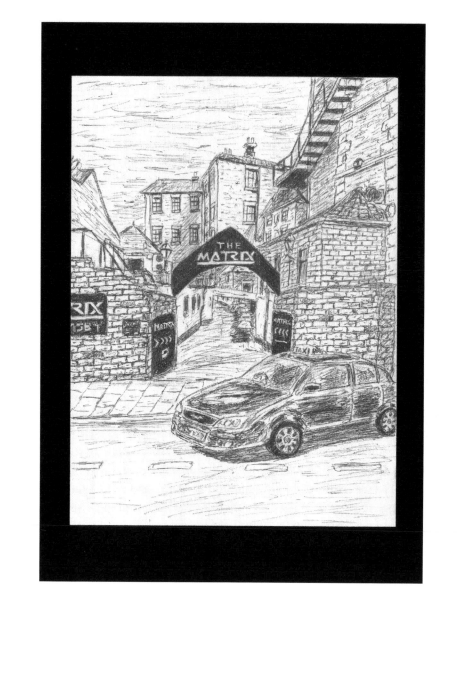

25694513R00148

Printed in Poland
by Amazon Fulfillment
Poland Sp. z o.o., Wrocław